Back to the Fajitas

A MEERA PATEL MYSTERY

LEENA CLOVER

Table of Contents

Chapter 1

Chapter 2

Chapter 3

Chapter 4

Chapter 5

Chapter 6

Chapter 7

Chapter 8

Chapter 9

Chapter 10

Chapter 11

Chapter 12

Chapter 13

Chapter 14

Chapter 15

Chapter 16

Chapter 17

Chapter 18

Chapter 19

Chapter 20

Chapter 21

Chapter 22

Chapter 23

Chapter 24

Chapter 25

Chapter 26

Chapter 27

Chapter 28

Chapter 29

Chapter 30

Chapter 31

Glossary

RECIPE - Masala Chai/ Chai Latte

RECIPE - Vegetable Puffs

RECIPE - Avocado Chili Salad

RECIPE - Chili Honey Corn

RECIPE - Bhel Poori

Join my Newsletter

Thank You

To road trips with the family

Back to the Fajitas

Chapter 1

I swallowed a big mouthful of my favorite breakfast and closed my eyes, savoring the smoky, spicy flavors. None of the Patels chomping on their meal had any inkling of what was to come.

Even with eyes closed, I knew what my grandpa was up to. He may be over 80, but he acts like a child most of the time.

"Put that butter down, Pappa!"

Pappa glared at me and cut off almost half a stick of butter in protest. He began slathering his thepla flatbread with it until every inch was dripping with melted butter. Motee Ba, my grandma, snatched the butter from him. She speared the buttery thepla with a fork and it landed in my brother Jeet's plate.

"Hansa!" my grandpa roared.

The gingham curtains in the kitchen window fluttered in the cool spring breeze. We were all gathered around the table for breakfast, and it was the usual mad scramble.

"Are you happy now, girl?" Pappa gave me the stink eye.

I ignored him and went on eating.

My name is Meera Patel and I am a 20 something girl from Swan Creek, Oklahoma. I live on the outskirts of town in our huge 6 bedroom ranch along with my extended family. We call this a 'joint family', where several generations try to coexist under the same roof. It's not easy by any account, but we do end up having fun.

"Settle down, Pappa," my Dad said as he walked in. "You need to watch your diet if you want to go with us."

My father is the head honcho at the electrical engineering department at Pioneer Polytechnic, our local university. He rarely involves himself in family matters. He never has time for small talk.

"Shut up, *gadhedo*," Pappa glared. "I'm going no matter what. I don't need your permission."

Pappa loves calling Dad an ass. It's almost become a nick name. The phone rang before Motee Ba could call him out for swearing.

"Hi Sylvie," she chirped.

"Is she baking our pies today?" Jeet asked eagerly.

Sylvie's pies are the talk of the county. And they are really that good. We never go anywhere without stocking up on some of them.

Motee Ba held up a hand, motioning Jeet to be quiet. Her face had turned ashen. The mood in the room changed as everyone noticed it one by one and stared at my grandma.

"We're just finishing breakfast," Motee Ba told Sylvie. "We'll be there soon."

I sprang up and gently guided her to a chair. I poured a glass of water and made her drink it. Motee Ba sat stunned, staring at the table.

"What is it?" Pappa leaned forward. "What's wrong, Hansa?"

Motee Ba looked at me and her eyes flickered. I got the message.

"Are you all done here?" I asked and started clearing the table. "Why don't you go watch TV, Pappa? Isn't Law & Order on right now?"

Pappa ignored me and tapped his cane.

"Don't treat me like a child, girl! Tell me what's wrong, Hansa. Tell me right now!"

"It's Charlie Gibson," Motee Ba barely whispered. "He's gone."

"But we're meeting for lunch today!" Pappa exclaimed. "Bet that no good boy dragged him off somewhere."

Then he realized what Motee Ba meant. His face blanched in

shock. Jeet sidled closer to him and put a hand on his shoulder.

Dad finally looked up and realized something was wrong.

"Sylvie heard from Audrey. She's going over there now with Jon."

Pappa stood up and tapped his cane.

"So are we. Get ready, Hansa!"

"I'll go with you," I offered, and Motee Ba nodded in relief.

The woman seated next to my Dad frowned. I understood.

"You don't have to come, Sally."

She had been quiet all this time. She didn't know Charlie Gibson. But she had a worried look on her face. She looked at Pappa and smiled reassuringly. Pappa seemed to take some comfort from it.

Pappa has a few old cronies in town. Charlie Gibson had been one of them. They were all in the twilight of their lives, so this type of news is kinda expected, I guess. But losing a friend is always hard. Pappa's temper is mercurial at best. I had no idea how he would take this sudden news.

I helped Motee Ba get ready and drove them to Charlie Gibson's house. There was a long line of cars and trucks in the cul de sac where Charlie's house was situated. News travels really fast in our town.

I spotted Jon and Sylvie's truck and frowned when I saw the car next to it. What was Stan Miller doing here? Then I spotted an ambulance with the lights off and my curiosity deepened.

Stan waddled out just as I finished helping Pappa and Motee Ba out of the car.

"Looks like a tough one, Meera," he plunged ahead without greeting us.

"Did his heart give out?" I asked tentatively.

"His heart gave out alright," Stan growled. "After he was stabbed to death."

"What do you mean?" I asked the stupid question.

"He was murdered," Stan said flatly. "No doubt about it."

"Meera," Motee Ba cried out as Pappa seemed to wobble.

I grabbed him tightly and coaxed him to sit inside the car. Sylvie and Jon came out, looking sad.

"It's best you don't go in there," she warned Motee Ba. "Not a pretty sight."

"I want to pay my respects," Pappa objected.

"They're sealing the place now anyway, Mr. Patel," Stan soothed. "This is a crime scene now."

"Can I have a look?" I asked.

"Do you really want to?" Stan pursed his lips.

I had been roped into solving a couple of murders earlier that year. But what was I thinking? I am not strong enough to stomach a gory crime scene.

"Maybe not," I agreed.

"You can pay your respects at the funeral," Jon coaxed Pappa.

"But we're leaving in a couple of days," he cried.

The entire Patel clan was embarking on an epic road trip for Spring Break. This was going to be a family caper, and Pappa was excited. We were going to drive all the way to the California coast to Sally's house, and take in some sights in between. Other than some trips to New Jersey to visit my aunt, or camping trips in the Oklahoma wilderness, we have never taken a family vacation. Everyone was looking forward to it.

"We'll think of something, don't worry," Sylvie patted Pappa. "I think it's best to leave now."

I shuffled everyone back in the car and followed Jon's truck to the diner.

Sylvie's Café & Diner is a fixture in our small town. The locals gather here for Sylvie's down home cooking. Her pies are legendary. It's also the place everyone congregates to get the latest scoop.

The parking lot was bursting and the hum of conversation could be heard outside. Becky, my best friend, was busy pouring coffee. She looked up when she saw us.

"You're back already?"

Sylvie ushered her into the kitchen and I followed.

"I'm glad you didn't go inside, child," Sylvie said to me. "And it was too much for your grandpa."

"Charlie Gibson was stabbed," I burst out, bringing Becky up to speed.

She almost dropped her coffee pot.

"Another murder? What's happening to this town?"

"Never mind that now," Sylvie ordered. "You girls get some good strong coffee for us. And those muffins I baked earlier. Let's get some sugar inside your grandpa, Meera."

I made Pappa eat the muffin and added real sugar to his coffee. He's a tea drinker so I had to force him to take a few sips.

"Why would anyone kill Charlie?" Pappa asked the question foremost on everyone's mind.

A few people turned to look at our table. I bet they were all talking about the same thing. The breakfast rush was over and the diner seemed too full for midweek.

"Vultures," Sylvie spat.

Sylvie's café had suffered from some false allegations. People had boycotted the diner not once but twice that year. These were the same people who had been eating at least one meal a day at Sylvie's for decades. Sylvie had been hurt deeply by the town's reaction.

"He was here yesterday," Jon supplied.

"He never missed my meatloaf," Sylvie said. "He was here at 12:30 every Tuesday, like clockwork."

"Did he seem well?" Motee Ba asked. "He didn't look sick?"

That didn't really matter in this case, but I kept my mouth shut.

"He was never sick in his life!" Pappa boomed. "Not a single day."

"It was that schedule he kept," Jon nodded. "Never seen anyone stick to routine like that."

A tear rolled down Pappa's eye.

"I bet it was that kid he took in. Told him it was a bad idea."

"We don't really know that for sure," Jon objected.

Pappa was referring to Leo Smith, an orphan Charlie had taken in a few months ago. No one knew anything about Leo. My grandpa had never warmed to the kid for some reason.

He flung a finger at me and bristled.

"You need to find out who did this, girl."

"Pappa," I objected. "The police are on the job. I'm sure they'll get to the bottom of it."

"Bah!" he roared. "We all know you're smarter than that Miller boy. I want justice for my friend."

My Dad and Pappa had both opposed my amateur sleuthing so far. I was sure he was speaking in the heat of the moment.

"Sure, Pappa," I said.

I had no intention of getting pulled into the affair. Spring Break was two days away and I was going to have a whale of a time, no matter what. I badly needed to unwind after the roller coaster ride my life had been for the past six months.

"So are you coming with us or not?" I asked Becky urgently,

pulling her away from the grownups.

"Not," Becky said glumly.

"Did Sylvie say no? I can talk to her."

"I haven't asked her."

I opened my mouth to protest but she warded me off.

"I'm not going to, Meera. You know the diner was shut down for a long time. I need to stay here and help Sylvie get it back on track."

"Now you're making me feel bad about the trip," I grumbled.

"You've helped us a lot already," Becky protested. "Chicken Curry Sundays are a hit and so are the samosa dumplings and the pakora fritters. You go have fun."

"I'll think of some more recipes on the road," I promised.

"You focus on spending time with Sally." Becky gave me a knowing look.

Sally Rossi had come into our lives suddenly this year. Her arrival had turned my life upside down, and I had tried to ignore her as much as I could. But my heart was slowly warming toward her, against my best intentions. My brain screamed and issued all kinds of dire warnings. But the glow in my heart was growing stronger.

She was my mother, after all.

Chapter 2

Sally had lunch ready for us when we got home. I warmed a big pot of tomato soup on the stove. Motee Ba was in the living room, trying to make small talk with Pappa.

Sally was buttering bread, layering them with cheese slices. None of us had an appetite that day and we just shoveled in some food to please Sally.

I drove to the gas station the moment I was done. Tony came out before I finished parking my car at the back. Tony Sinclair is my best friend in this world. More so than Becky but I won't admit it in front of her. I think she knows anyway.

Tony's mother comes from Mumbai in India, or Bombay as she refers to it. I call her Aunt Reema, but Tony's no cousin of mine. I had a big crush on him in high school. Then we went our separate ways, all set to slay the world. Fate had brought us back to Swan Creek. We are very close now, close friends. We are not ready to consider anything more, at least not right now.

All said, I can't imagine life without Tony.

"You didn't go in there, did you?" he asked worriedly, pulling me into a tight hug.

I knew what he was talking about. The town grapevine must have been working overtime.

"Stan said it wasn't a pretty sight."

"And you did the sensible thing for a change?" Tony asked in disbelief.

"It's not that. I don't want anything to spoil our trip."

"You can't brush off what happened, Meera. Charlie Gibson's no more. How's your grandpa taking it?"

"He wants me to work on it," I burst out. "Can you imagine? After all the grief he gave me for trying to find Jyothi!"

"Don't tell me you're considering it?" Tony's face fell. "I'm really looking forward to Vegas."

"Don't worry, Tony. Nothing's coming between us and this road trip."

We high fived each other, excited about the trip. So it wasn't going to be some wild drunken sortie like you saw in the movies. But I was fine with that. We were going to have fun with the family, a different kind of fun.

"So what's Becky going to do?" Tony asked.

"She's staying back. So it's just the one car for us."

"Sounds like a hoot," Tony smiled.

"Oh no!" I moaned. "Squashed in a car with Pappa for hours together?"

"Don't worry. We'll be stopping every other hour."

We talked about the trip for a while and my mood improved. I drove to work and stayed until late to make up for my hours. I walked to the food court around 6 to grab a bite before they closed. I caught a glimpse of someone familiar as I bit into my burger.

"Leo!" I called out.

He didn't turn back.

I was almost sure the fleeting figure had belonged to Leo Smith. But what was he doing out here on the Pioneer campus? That too on the day he had lost his benefactor?

I was asleep on my feet by the time I reached home. It was almost 10. Sally was sitting in the kitchen with Motee Ba. She stood up and started warming up some food for me.

"Is that the shopping list?" I asked Motee Ba after gulping down my dinner.

She nodded.

"Your mother and I will go to the city and get most of this tomorrow. Let me know if you want to add something."

I skimmed over the items. Everything from chewing gum to batteries was listed on it.

"Toilet paper? We are going to stay in hotels, Motee Ba. Good hotels."

"You never know with those rest areas," she said. "Better to be prepared."

Judging by the mile long list, we were prepared for the Apocalypse.

"Becky's not coming so I guess we'll be taking the LX."

Motee Ba's face lit up.

"We'll all fit right in."

The LX is a behemoth, but seven people in a car is a bit too much, if you ask me. Better than playing tag on the Interstate though. When we take multiple cars, half the time is spent in wondering where the other car is.

I dragged my feet at work the next day, counting the hours until Spring Break. The campus was emptying pretty fast, and groups of college kids could be seen hurrying around dropping names like Cancun and Acapulco.

I stopped at Sylvie's after work.

"How's your grandpa doing?" she asked the moment she saw me.

I shrugged. I hadn't had a chance to call home during the day.

"Haven't you talked to Motee Ba today?" I asked her.

Sylvie shook her head.

"Honey and your mother have gone shopping."

"Oh yeah," I remembered.

Pappa must have been alone at home all day.

"I better go and check on him, Sylvie."

Sylvie waved me off and I sped home.

Pappa was outside, pacing in the yard. The weather was milder than winter but there was a nip in the air. What was he doing out in the cold?

I took his arm and nudged him inside.

"They should have been home by now," he muttered.

His hand was almost frozen.

"Why don't I make some tea?"

My grandpa can make tea in the microwave but he doesn't like it that way. I made Masala Chai the traditional Gujarati way, just the way he drank it.

He sat at the kitchen table, smacking his lips.

It was way past his tea time. My family is used to having some heavy snacks with their afternoon tea. We eat dinner late around 9 PM.

"What do you want to eat, Pappa?"

He was quiet. I decided to make some vegetable puffs to cheer him up.

I set out the puff pastry from the fridge and washed some frozen peas. It was too early for peas from our garden. I pulsed peas in the Cuisinart along with some garlic. Luckily, there were some boiled potatoes in the refrigerator. I rolled out the pastry and soon my puffs were in the oven.

Jeet came in and looked around.

"Are you making some chicken puffs?" he asked.

"Not today," I said. "Where have you been? Couldn't you get Pappa his tea?"

"I asked him. He said no."

Jeet went out to watch some TV. Pappa sat in his chair, looking gloomy. I didn't know what to say. There was nothing I could do to console him.

The oven dinged and I heard a car outside. Pappa tapped his cane and started to get up. Sally came in with her arms full of stuff, followed by Motee Ba. Jeet was dispatched to help them unload the car.

I set out the steaming puffs and pulled out bottles of chili sauce and tamarind chutney. The Masala tea was poured and the ladies sighed with relief.

"That was some trip," Motee Ba said, taking a long sip of her tea.

Sally nodded and smiled. There's a pattern to her smiles. I can almost decipher them now. She was agreeing with Motee Ba.

Pappa finally ate some puffs and drank his tea. He bounced back with a burst of energy.

"Did you get everything on the list?" he demanded.

Motee Ba looked apologetic.

"Well, we forgot the Doritos."

My grandpa made a rude sound.

"Who needs that orange dust anyway?" He gave me a quelling look. "Ten days on the road – you better eat homemade snacks as much as you can."

"We'll start cooking for the trip tomorrow," Motee Ba promised him.

They had come up with a list of stuff that would last a few days. We made short work of the puffs, even the second batch. I set a couple aside for Dad.

I thought about Charlie Gibson as I came out of the shower. The phone rang and it was Stan Miller.

"Hey Stan," I said with bated breath.

For the first time, I wasn't keen on getting the skinny from him.

"We just got the preliminary autopsy report. It was the knife alright. He died almost instantly."

"He didn't try to defend himself?" I asked.

"Doesn't look like it," Stan said. "He was stabbed from the back. I don't think Charlie even had time to turn around."

"So you think it was someone he knew? How did he let someone get that close?"

Charlie Gibson wasn't an extrovert. I doubt anyone other than his housekeeper or Leo ever entered his house.

"That, or the person was very stealthy. Charlie didn't hear him, obviously."

"What about Bandit?"

"Charlie's mutt?" Stan asked. "I didn't think of that."

Stan sometimes overlooks obvious things. Okay, he often overlooks the obvious. At least he owns up to it nowadays.

"Where was he this morning?"

"In the hallway between the kitchen and his bedroom."

"Was he all riled up?"

"Wake up, Meera. He was dead!"

"Who, Bandit?"

"No, Charlie Gibson!"

"I'm talking about the dog. Where was the dog when you went into the house today?"

"I don't know. I didn't notice. Maybe someone let him out."

"How come he wasn't barking all night?"

I heard the sound of pen scratching on paper.

"Let me find out," Stan said.

I held myself back. I didn't want to get involved.

"So…you're leaving on this trip of yours?"

"Oh yes! We are all going."

"You were a big help on the last two cases," Stan mumbled. "I'm sort of used to discussing stuff with you."

Was Stan Miller finally giving me a compliment?

"I guess we can talk on the phone," I said grudgingly.

"Do you have a cell phone?" he asked.

He knew I didn't. He was angling for Dad's cell phone number. There was no way I was sharing that with him.

"You know I don't, Stan. I'll have to call you myself when we check into our hotel at night."

Stan thanked me for the offer.

"You can always send me a message via Becky."

Stan hung up and I went to bed, not sure of what I had signed up for.

Charlie Gibson's memorial service was to be held in Sylvie's Café on Friday night. She made it happen just so Pappa could attend. He had lost most of his enthusiasm for the trip.

"Why don't you say something at the memorial service, Pappa?" I asked.

Maybe talking about his friend would be cathartic.

"You mean like a eulogy?" he asked. "I'm not much of a speaker, Meera."

"What are you saying, Mr. Patel? Don't you remember all those speeches you gave at the mill?"

"That was fifty years ago, Hansa. I'm old now."

I left them arguing over it.

"Good call, Meera," Dad patted me on the back as he went into his office.

He must have heard me talking to Pappa. Dad had been closeted in his office like it was the end of the world. He had never taken a one week break from work. That's what academia does to you - one of the reasons I stay away from being a professor.

I put in a load of laundry and thought about meeting Leo at the memorial. I wanted to ask him why he'd ignored me at the food court.

Chapter 3

Leo Smith stood just inside the entrance to Sylvie's, greeting people as they arrived for Charlie's memorial service. The days were lengthening, and the sky was streaked orange and pink near the horizon. It was 6 PM and it had been a long day. We had an early start planned for next morning. But there was no way we would miss this final farewell to Charlie Gibson.

"Thanks for coming, Mr. Patel," Leo shook Pappa's hand. "Charlie would have wanted you here."

"Don't tell me what he would or would not have wanted, boy!" Pappa boomed. "Known him a lot longer than you."

Pappa can sound really gruff at times, but he was just putting on a front.

Leo bowed his head but remained silent. His eyes were swollen and red rimmed. His gray eyes seemed to have sunk deeper in the last two days. There were dark circles under his eyes. Whatever Pappa thought about him, Leo was grieving.

I patted him on the back and ushered Pappa to a table. Jon came over to talk to him. Sylvie had arranged a buffet table at one end. I handed her a Crockpot full of queso and a bag of tortilla chips. I spied some corn bread and a pan of fried chicken. Baskets of muffins vied for space with cookie platters and casseroles.

Small town life has a certain pattern. Casseroles are du jour for a house of mourning. I doubted if anyone had cared about taking food to Leo. They wouldn't turn up empty handed at a public place though.

Dad and Sally arrived just after us and gave their condolences. Tony arrived with Aunt Reema. He made a line for the buffet table. I got up to join him.

"Looks like you're loading up for tomorrow," I teased, eyeing Tony's heaped plate. "You know we're not going on a walking trip, right?"

"Skipped lunch," he said through bites of fried chicken.

Almost everyone had arrived and people were settling in at their tables. Leo still stood by the door, lost in thought.

I filled a plate and took it to him.

"I'm not hungry," he shook his head.

"When was the last time you ate?" I reasoned. "You need to keep your strength up."

Tears flew down Leo's cheeks. He turned away, trying to hide his grief. I put the plate down and hugged him tightly. He returned my hug with fervor. I had a nasty suspicion. I was probably the first person who had hugged him since Charlie's death.

"Charlie was so good to me," he sobbed. "He was a kind man. I can never repay him for what he did for me."

"You made him happy, Leo," I consoled.

"I wasn't there for him," Leo said through his tears. "Not when it mattered, when he needed me."

Charlie Gibson had walked into Sylvie's one Saturday morning a few months ago, accompanied by a tall, skinny kid. His unruly mop of hair needed a cut and his clothes had seen one wash too many. Charlie introduced him to everyone.

"This is Leo. He'll be living with me now."

No one knew where Leo Smith had come from or who he was. Some said he was a long lost relative of Charlie's. Some said he was a foundling. Others were sure he was a punk who just got out of juvie. The gossips wondered if there would be a sudden influx of drugs in Swan Creek. All kinds of nasty things were whispered.

Charlie Gibson ignored it all. Leo Smith did not enroll in school, fueling the rumors. We later learned he was home schooling himself. Charlie Gibson had lived in Swan Creek for the last fifty years. He had been alone since his wife died twenty years ago. He was declared senile by the people's court and they decided to turn a blind eye to Leo Smith as long as he didn't disturb the peace in town.

Leo surprised everyone by his model behavior. He turned out to be a loner. His life was as regimented as Charlie's, but he didn't seem to mind. He was often seen at the library, absorbed in his books. Charlie brought him to Sylvie's for Sunday dinner sometimes. Other than that, we hardly came across Leo Smith.

I made sure Leo ate a few bites. He made a short speech thanking everyone for coming.

"We're here for Charlie," someone muttered.

Pappa gave a speech after that.

I wondered where Leo was going to live now.

"You're one brave soul, Leo, living in that house alone."

"I don't have a choice," he said sadly. "I can't go anywhere while the police are investigating."

I wondered if Charlie Gibson had any heirs. I cringed at the thought of some obscure relative driving Leo out. I decided to talk to Sylvie about it.

Then I remembered what Leo had said a few minutes ago.

I caught his eye and went into the pantry. He followed me in, his face quizzical.

"What did you mean you weren't there?" I asked.

"I was out of town that night. I drove to Ponca City to meet some friends. I was going to stay with them for a day or two."

"I didn't know you have friends in the area?"

"I don't," Leo said. "They are driving through, going south to Corpus Christi and then on to Florida, maybe. I just wanted to spend some time with them."

Spring Break was rolling across the country so that kind of made sense. I was itching to ask Leo where these friends were from. That might give me an idea of where he came from.

"We're going on a road trip too," I told Leo, "all the way to California."

His face fell.

"I was hoping you'd be here helping the cops."

"I don't work for them, Leo. I was just trying to help a friend out."

He looked like he wanted to say something but was too shy to voice it.

"Is there something you want to tell me?"

I prayed it wasn't a confession.

He hesitated.

"As long as you are in the right, I'll try to help you."

"Well, Charlie and I talked about how the cops almost arrested you once. And your friend." He tipped his head toward Sylvie. "What if they zero in on me?"

He looked like the kid he was, helpless and uncertain.

"I don't know too many people in this town, Meera."

I didn't want to make any false promises. But I could see Leo was barely holding it together.

"You can always send me a message. You know Becky, don't you? I'll be calling her from the road."

Leo gave me a watery smile. I called Becky over and introduced her to Leo.

"Of course I know Leo," she exclaimed. "He's come here plenty of times with Charlie."

I told Becky she was to pass on any message Leo wanted to send me. That seemed to satisfy him.

He took my hands in his. "Can you promise me something? Find out who did this. I know Charlie was your grandpa's friend. He trusted you, Meera. He was really proud of the way you solved those two cases."

I grudgingly made a promise, sounding as noncommittal as I could.

Stan Miller came in and made a beeline toward me. I asked Leo to get me a cookie from the table.

"It's beginning to look like a robbery gone bad," he whispered.

Charlie Gibson wasn't exactly swimming in money. He was a retired man living on a fixed income. I let Stan continue.

"A couple of drawers have been pulled out from a desk, and his wallet was on the floor near a window."

"How much money do you think he had, Stan?" I rolled my eyes.

"Doesn't have to be much. It's all about how urgently someone needs it."

Stan walked to the buffet and began loading his plate. He can't ignore a loaded table for long.

"Never did a thing out of turn," someone was saying. "He had a solid routine, Mr. Gibson did. There was a day to go to the library, and a day for the bank. And he never switched the days come hell or high water."

Audrey Jones was talking to some other older ladies between bites of Sylvie's banana cream pie. The short woman wasn't wearing her trademark smock for a change. How did she know about Charlie's habits?

"Kid's taking it real hard," she said under her breath. "He's either really cut up or a very good actor."

"What do we really know about him?" A frazzled older woman quipped.

She had been standing in Charlie's yard when we drove over on that fateful day.

"That's Anna Collins," Becky supplied, handing me a slice of pecan pie. "Saved the last slice for you."

Sylvie had packed a few pies for us to take along, but I wasn't saying no to a slice.

"Who's she?"

"Charlie's neighbor. Lives two doors down. And that's his housekeeper."

"Who, Audrey? I didn't know she worked for Charlie?"

Becky gave me a look.

"She's been working for Charlie Gibson since his wife died. If you want to know anything about Charlie's habits, she's your guy."

I didn't take the bait. But I was beginning to sense a pattern. I hoped Leo Smith had a thick skin.

I went and sat at our table.

"Are you all packed and ready to leave bright and early?" Aunt Reema winked.

"Don't know about the kids," Motee Ba said, smiling at us, "but we are ready."

Pappa gave us the stink eye.

"We are leaving at 6 AM and not a moment later."

That was going to happen.

"I wish you were coming," I told Auntie Reema.

"Do you want to take my car?" she laughed.

She knows me well.

"We are all going in that big Lexus," Pappa said stonily. "Why do you think your father spent a ridiculous amount of money on it?"

Dad had bought the big SUV against Pappa's wishes. Frugality is ingrained in us Patels. A car that gave less than 10 miles per gallon and sat in the garage most of the time was a big waste of money according to my grandpa.

"The back seat can get a bit cramped," Jeet ventured.

Pappa tapped his cane.

"We are all going in one car, as a family."

"Have you looked at the time?" Motee Ba stepped in. "I think we should leave now."

We said goodbye to Leo. I had a weird feeling wash over me. Would he be here when we came back?

"Here's my email," I said, scribbling my email id on a slip of paper. "Keep in touch, Leo."

His eyes filled up and I pulled him in a hug again.

"Don't be a stranger, you hear?"

Motee Ba told him the same thing and the grownups stepped out to Dad's car. I spotted Sylvie going into her office. I remembered what I wanted to tell her.

"Don't worry, Meera. Our door's always open for him. I already told him that. He's not going to be abandoned again."

I trust Sylvie as much as I trust my family. So I was relieved.

I stopped at Tony's on the way home.

"Why aren't you home yet, Meera?" he asked me.

"Why aren't you?"

I started loading up on candy bars.

"Didn't Granny's list have candy on it?"

"This is my secret stash."

"Go home!" Tony said, pushing me toward the door. "We have to start at 6 AM sharp."

We both burst out laughing. Then I sobered as I thought of Leo.

"Did you hear those people at the diner? Looks like Leo's been convicted without trial. Everyone's pointing the finger at him."

"I'm not worried. He's got you in his corner."

I flung my arms wide.

"You too? Have you forgotten we are leaving tomorrow?"

"You'll think of something," Tony said seriously.

Was I worthy of the faith these people had in me?

Chapter 4

The alarm snapped me awake at 4:30 AM. I hit the Snooze button and snuggled under the covers. There was a loud rapping on my room door.

"Time to get up," Dad yelled from the other side.

There was a series of such raps to be heard through the house. I scrambled up and rushed into the shower. We were having breakfast on the road, but we couldn't start without coffee.

Motee Ba was filling large travel mugs with the hot brew. Sally poured juice in paper cups and handed them out. The tart orange finally took away any remaining drowsiness. Pappa was at the front door, muttering about the time.

"Relax, Mr. Patel," Motee Ba told him. "This is a vacation, not some kind of drill. You have to stop looking at the time now."

He made a rude noise and ignored her.

Tony's truck pulled up in the driveway and he bounded in, smelling of Zest soap.

"Start loading the cars, kids," Dad ordered.

Jeet, Tony and I spent half an hour trying to get everything in the trunk. Dad had strictly capped us off at one bag per person. We would have to do laundry somewhere along the way. There were ten bags of food and a few more for essentials.

Finally, all the windows were double checked and the house was locked. I knew what was coming next. Pappa hobbled toward the car. He didn't have to call shotgun. He just glared at everyone, daring us to contradict him.

"You can sit in the front now, Pappa, but you'll have to take turns sitting in the back."

Pappa ignored Dad and tried to get in on his own. The seat was higher so Tony had to help him in.

"Can I drive?" Jeet asked.

"Maybe later," Dad said, giving me a look.

Jeet was going to pester us like this all the way, but he would have to wait a month of Sundays before anyone let him get behind the wheel. He was shuffled into the third row along with me. Dad, Sally and Motee Ba sat in the second row and Tony took the wheel.

We said a small prayer and set off.

"Don't cross the speed limit, boy!" Pappa growled.

Tony took his time getting used to the different buttons and dials on the dash. By the time he merged onto the Interstate, he was handling the car well.

"When are we stopping for breakfast?" Jeet asked. "I'm hungry."

It was barely 6:30 AM and there was a glow on the horizon. We watched the orange ball of the sun come up slowly. Sally handed Jeet an apple. Then she started cutting them and handed out slices in disposable plates.

The road trip had begun and we let out a cheer.

Tony made good time and pulled into a Denny's in Oklahoma City. Everyone scrambled out as soon as they could. We had our fill of eggs and pancakes and got back on the road.

"How about some music?" Dad said, handing Tony a CD.

"You burned a disc?" I asked.

The LX cut through the miles and everyone dozed off a bit. Pappa was snoring.

"I need you here," Tony mouthed at me in the rearview mirror. "Next to me."

I shrugged. Wasn't much I could do about it at that moment.

I nodded off for a few minutes myself and dreamt of Charlie Gibson. He had been one of the first people to try my Masala

Fried Chicken.

"You know I am pretty set in my ways, Meera," he warned. "But I always like to encourage young people."

He took a bite and gasped as the chili hit him. Then his taste buds adjusted to the unfamiliar spices and he began enjoying it.

"You've got a winner here," he had nodded at Sylvie. "Give these stodgy townsfolk something to talk about."

The car veered off the shoulder onto a rumble strip and snapped me awake.

"Are you tired already?" I teased Tony.

Everyone moved around in their limited space and a pit stop was called for.

"We're coming up on a rest area soon," Tony said, squinting at a road sign.

The rest area wasn't very good and it had no restrooms. Tony looked for a way to enter the town. He finally stopped at a big gas station. I desperately needed an icy drink.

"Anybody want anything? I'm getting a Coke."

"We've got a big bottle of cola with us, Meera. Just get some ice."

I rolled my eyes at Motee Ba.

"We are on the road for over a week, Meera. Plenty of time to buy what you want."

I got six large cups of ice, and paid a few cents for each one. Tony and I strolled around at the back, sipping our drinks. I was thinking about Leo.

"What's wrong?" Tony asked.

He can sense my mood.

"People are talking about Leo. It's just like the time Sylvie was blackballed for her pie."

"It's just talk, Meera."

"And we know how damaging it can be. They are not saying anything specific. Just hinting at something vague."

"You've got Stan's ear this time. If the police think Leo's a suspect, you'll know soon enough."

I processed that and decided there was nothing I could do about it.

I took the wheel and Tony sat next to me. Pappa grumbled all the way into the back. Everyone ignored him.

"Are we still in Oklahoma?" Jeet asked.

"Sure, we are," Dad said. "We're on Route 66 now. It's a historic route. Very famous. You must have read about it at school."

Jeet managed to evade the question. He had never crossed state lines by road. So this was a new experience for him.

"You know those signs we see when we leave our county?" Dad said. "You'll see similar signs when we cross the state border. So you'll know when you leave Oklahoma and enter Texas."

"Okay!" Jeet sat up. "When will that happen?"

"Why don't you check this map and tell me?"

Dad got busy quizzing Jeet on his map reading skills.

We made a quick stop at the next rest area on Pappa's request and drove on. The LX handled beautifully and I felt a sense of euphoria, up in the high cabin with heated seats warming my heiny. There were patches of old snow dusting the land and bushes and temperatures were in the 50s. Not bad for spring.

"Welcome to Texas," Jeet cried out, pointing at a green sign by the side of the road. "Drive Friendly! You hear that Meera?"

Jeet almost jumped in his seat with excitement and banged his head against the roof of the car. Tony and I burst out laughing.

"How old are you, 5?" I smirked.

"This calls for a snack," Pappa declared.

Sally brought out paper cups and Motee Ba filled them with *chevdo*, an Indian snack made with rice flakes, peanuts and lots of stuff. Something like a pub mix. As if we didn't have enough things to eat, a package had arrived the day before from my aunt. She had special ordered an array of Gujarati snacks, knowing how Pappa wasn't too crazy about pretzels and stuff. My Aunt Anita must have spent a small fortune on the shipping fees.

Tony and I shared a cup and I dipped in it after putting the car on Cruise Control.

"Keep your eyes on the road," Pappa reminded me from the back.

"You're missing Becky, aren't you?" Motee Ba asked sagely.

I told her what we had talked about.

"The diner's suffered a lot this year. Let's hope Leo doesn't face the same fate."

"I promised Charlie I would keep an eye on him," Pappa said as he swallowed another mouthful of *chevdo*.

He held a hand out imperiously and Sally placed a glass of water in it. Pappa doesn't drink from bottles. I waited for more as he gulped down the water noisily.

"When did you do that Pappa?" I asked.

"Every time we met, girl!"

I almost whipped my head around.

"Are you saying he had some kind of intuition about dying?"

"He was 75. At that age, every day is a gift."

"He didn't feel threatened by anyone?"

"Charlie kept to himself most of the time," Pappa said. "We met for lunch once a month. Why would anyone want to harm him?"

"That's the million dollar question, isn't it?" Tony said. "If we know that, we'll know who killed him."

"Why are you talking about this now?" Dad complained. "We're on vacation."

Sally patted Dad's arm. Or maybe I imagined it. Apparently, Dad didn't know Pappa wanted me to find Charlie's killer. We had made good time inspite of all the stops. We had lunch at a big rest stop, gorging on *thepla* flatbread, pickles, yogurt and fruit cocktail. We cut one of Sylvie's pies for dessert.

An hour later, I pulled into our hotel in Amarillo.

"Let's freshen up and get going right away," I said. "We need to catch the sunset at the canyon."

Palo Duro Canyon lies to the south of Amarillo and is one of the attractions of the area. There was also a historic Route 66 District. We planned to go there for dinner.

"Aren't we going to the Grand Canyon?" Jeet asked. "Why are we going to one more canyon?"

Pappa and Jeet stayed back and the rest of us went to the canyon. We did the tourist thing, enjoying the scenic drive, stopping at scenic overlooks, taking pictures.

Sally pointed out the juniper bushes, and the sage and yucca. She and Dad went off, whispering to each other. I took Motee Ba's arm and led her to a bench at an overlook. It had a nice view of the canyon.

We were quiet for a while, soaking in the view. I thought I saw a Palo Duro mouse and a wild turkey. Wild flowers were beginning to bloom in some places. In a few weeks, they would form a colorful carpet across the canyon.

"Your Pappa's taking this hard," Motee Ba said to me. "He never liked Leo much. But now he's worried about him."

"About that…" I wondered how to say what I was thinking.

"You know, Motee Ba, Jeet will be off to college soon. Maybe we can ask Leo to come live with us for a while."

Motee Ba's face lit up.

"You wouldn't mind having him underfoot?"

"He seems like a good kid," I reasoned, trying to sound casual. "How old is he anyway? He'll go to college soon, won't he?"

Motee Ba sprang up, looking excited.

"I talked to Sylvie. She'll take him in now, and he can be with them over the summer. He can come to us in the fall."

Motee Ba is a grandma after all. We were all secretly dreading the void in our lives after Jeet went to college. Having a young boy to feed and pamper sounded like the perfect antidote.

"Now I have to talk to Sally," Motee Ba plotted, rubbing her hands. "Once she's on board, Andy will fall in line."

"Sally's a guest herself. You don't need to ask her."

"Your mother's not a guest, Meera," Motee Ba laughed. "When are you going to accept it?"

"Accept her, you mean," I mumbled.

My grandma kissed the top of my head and ignored me. We walked around, stretching our legs, and headed back to the hotel.

Chapter 5

We were all longing for a hot meal that night. I was worn out from the day on the road, but it was a good kind of tired. The days stretched ahead, promising new sights and new experiences.

"Is there an Indian restaurant in this town?" Pappa asked.

"Mr. Patel, you have promised to give the local food a chance," Motee Ba reminded him. "Don't mention Indian food until we reach Vegas."

Pappa was the only finicky eater of the lot. The rest of us were eager to taste the big and bold flavors of Texas food. I had done some research and made a list of local specialties.

"Where are we going, Meera?" Dad asked.

"This place has been around for over 50 years. They started on the old Route 66 and then moved to this new spot when the Interstate was built."

Tony and I tried some local beers and talked Dad into trying one. Pappa stuck to his Scotch. We dug into the hand breaded mushrooms and onion rings, waiting for our entrees. Pappa liked the spicy chicken quesadilla. Tony and Jeet dug into steaks. Motee Ba shared Pappa's meal and I enjoyed a juicy burger. Sally ordered side salads for everyone.

"We'll be eating out every day," Motee Ba warned. "Need to get those veggies in."

Tony and I dropped everyone off and drove to Walmart. We were stocking up on water and fresh fruit on Sally's orders.

"Are you going to call Stan today?" Tony asked.

"We just met him yesterday. I don't think he must have done a lot since then. Do you?"

Tony, Jeet and I were sharing a huge room with three queen beds. I called Becky from my room using a calling card. Tony hadn't offered me the use of his cell phone, and I wasn't going to ask him for it.

"Where have you been, Meera?" she almost screamed in my ear. "I've been waiting for your call."

"Okay, okay, I missed you too."

I wondered why Becky sounded so anxious.

"Have you talked to Stan?" she burst out.

"Not yet. I wanted to catch up with you first."

She clammed up.

"What is it, Becks? Something wrong?"

"How was your day? Is everyone alright?"

"We had fun, and we missed you," I told her. "Everyone's fine. Probably asleep by now. We had a big dinner, Texas style."

"Good for you," Becky said.

I sensed her hesitation.

"What are you not telling me?"

"The cops think Leo has been joyriding."

"He went to Ponca City to visit some friends," I said defensively. "He told me that last night."

"Well, Charlie's wallet was empty so there was money missing from it. They think Leo stole that money."

"Is there a reason for them to think that?"

"It's what his kind does," Becky wailed. "That's what people are saying."

"What rot is this now, Becky?"

"Leo wanted money so he grabbed what he got and ran off. After he stabbed Charlie, that is."

"That's ridiculous."

I sucked in a deep breath. I had a hard time imagining Leo doing any such thing.

"That's what they're all saying. Maybe you'll get the real scoop from Stan."

It was almost 10 PM. I promised to keep Becky posted and dialed Stan's number. He answered immediately.

"Hello?" he asked tentatively. "Is that you, Meera?"

"Hey Stan! Looks like you've been busy."

"So you know? You won't tell him, right?"

"What are you talking about, Stan?"

"We are arresting Leo Smith for Charlie Gibson's murder."

I waved a hand in the air, trying to grab Tony's attention. The hotel phone didn't have a speaker so Tony huddled close to me trying to listen in.

"Why do you think he's guilty?" I tried to remain calm.

"Money's missing from Charlie's wallet. A neighbor saw someone sneaking out of a window. We know Charlie was stabbed from behind. He trusted his killer enough to turn his back on him. Who else could it be but Leo?"

"How much money are we talking about here?"

"We are not sure. We are assuming he had some cash on hand for every day expenses."

"So we're talking about what, fifty bucks?"

"Maybe not even that, Meera."

"And you think Leo actually murdered Charlie for that?"

"Well, he must have needed gas money. Where was he going to get it? He doesn't have a job. He did chores around the house – mowed the lawn and stuff. But Charlie didn't pay him for it."

"Leo took Charlie's car. It could have had a full tank already."

"One of the bills in Leo's wallet had something written on it. Cashier at the bank remembers handing it out to Charlie."

"Aren't you missing something obvious? Maybe Charlie just gave it to Leo, knowing he wanted to go meet his friends."

"There is no proof of that."

"But you have proof that he stole it?"

"I told you, this neighbor almost swears she saw Leo jump out of the window."

"What does Leo say about it?"

"We haven't asked him about it yet. We'll question him tomorrow."

Something didn't feel right. Tony whispered in my ear, and I struck my palm against my forehead.

"Say he's guilty. Why did he come back?"

"I don't know," Stan said stonily.

"Would you come back if you were guilty?"

"Maybe he's overconfident. He thinks he can get away with it."

I sighed. I was too tired to process it.

"Keep me posted, please."

"Do you have any other theories, Meera?"

I didn't, because I hadn't spared a thought for Charlie Gibson. I wasn't too happy with the way things were going.

"Not right now, Stan."

He said goodbye and hung up.

"Can you imagine that?" I burst out, following Tony as he paced around the room.

Jeet had been flicking the channels on the TV.

"Is this your latest project?" he asked, making quotes around the word project.

"You have no idea how hard life is for Leo, do you?" I attacked Jeet. "Count your blessings, young one. You will soon experience the big bad world and then you'll realize how lucky you are."

"Yeah, man!" Tony said, shaking his head at Jeet in disgust.

His expression said Jeet had broken some bro code. Jeet sobered, switched off the light over his bed, and disappeared under the covers.

Tony and I stepped outside with unspoken agreement. The parking lot stretched into darkness. We have our share of large empty lots in Swan Creek but this was something else. We walked in a line toward the edge of the hotel's property. The sky was inky black, and the stars shone bright.

"You got most of that, right?" I asked Tony.

He looked grim.

"Pappa's going to be shocked. He might even ask us to turn back."

"I don't really know Leo," Tony admitted. "I've hardly spoken to him a few times."

"You want to know why I believe he is innocent."

I can guess what Tony's thinking too. Tony nodded, walking on with his hands in his pockets.

"I don't know much about him either. None of us do. Who is he? Where did Charlie find him? Why did he bring him home? We know nothing."

I wasn't the only one who trusted Leo. Sylvie and Motee Ba were ready to offer him a home. That had to count for something. They were way more experienced in the ways of the world. And they had opened their hearts to Leo.

"It's just instinct," I told Tony. "Some kind of gut feeling. I think Leo's innocent."

"He couldn't have a better advocate than Meera Patel."

Tony put an arm around my shoulder, hugging me close. We went in, finally feeling the exhaustion from the day catch up with us.

The next morning, I stayed in bed until Tony and Jeet were done with their showers. Then I grabbed a quick one and dressed in layers. We would be crossing into New Mexico today. I wore a turquoise top and a leather jacket. I was looking forward to buying some nice silver and turquoise jewelry to match the outfit.

"This place has the best pancakes," Dad was exclaiming.

He has a sweet tooth the size of Texas. We all do. Jeet and Dad were looking at some flyers at the front desk.

"The guy at the desk recommends it," Dad stressed. "Always trust the locals."

It was 7:30 AM and Pappa was fuming because we were late.

"Calm down, Pappa!" Dad finally glared at him. "We're on vacation. 7:30 is early enough. We'll hit the road by 9. We won't be driving more than 4-5 hours a day anyway."

Everyone ordered the pancakes. We also got eggs and grits and bacon. The hash browns were made fresh, crispy and burnt at the edges. Dad was driving today. Sally got in next to him. Tony and I sat in the third row. Once again, I wished we had brought a second car.

Motee Ba was the last to get in. She had been talking to Sylvie on the phone. She caught my eye and I realized she had the latest intel.

"They are talking to him now," she whispered.

That meant the police had brought Leo in for questioning. Would they arrest him today?

"What are you talking about, Hansa?" Pappa asked loudly.

Dad looked at us through the rearview mirror.

"Why don't we forget about Swan Creek and home for a while?" he said. "This is our first vacation since you kids grew up. Just enjoy the ride."

I got the message. Dad didn't want to talk about Charlie Gibson or Leo. He was giving me a subtle warning. My Dad is pretty cool most of the time. But when he puts his foot down, you better fall in line.

"What was the last vacation we took with Mom?" Jeet asked.

He's become an expert at sucking up to Sally. Sally was missing from our life for several years. Her sudden reappearance had thrown me off. Jeet had easily accepted her as our long lost mother. I wasn't ready to do that yet.

"You were too young, kiddo," Dad said, smiling fondly at Sally.

Too young to remember, he meant. But Sally didn't remember either. Dad launched into the story of a weekend trip we had taken into the Ozark mountains. This must have been just a few weeks before Sally went away.

Our trip was truly monumental, considering. I decided to take Dad's advice and cleared my mind. I looked out of the window at the changing landscape. We hit a bank of fog just outside Amarillo. It started raining, giving us a firsthand experience of the infamous panhandle weather.

I wanted to be there for Leo Smith. But I didn't know how I was going to manage that from a distance. I would just have to try harder.

Chapter 6

The LX blazed through the rain and sleet and we made good time. We stopped in a small town at a gas station. We huddled under an awning, sipping hot chocolate, taking in the desolate countryside. Other than the semis thundering across the Interstate, there wasn't much to be seen.

"Your Pappa's not going to like it," Motee Ba told me.

"We'll know more when I talk to Stan later tonight."

Motee Ba looked distressed.

"Why do you believe Leo is innocent?"

Motee Ba was quiet. "Charlie usually kept people at arm's length. But he trusted Leo. He must have seen something in the kid."

The sky cleared up after that and the car cut through the miles rapidly. A demand for snacks had been made and we had dipped into the stuff my aunt sent. There were some chips made from black eyed peas. The road stretched ahead as far as the eye could see. The landscape was barren, with some sparse dry grass and open fields. A water tower would loom up suddenly, indicating we were passing a small town.

There was a lull in the car until Jeet suddenly cried out.

"Welcome to New Mexico!"

There was a cheer as we entered the second state since leaving home. Dad spotted the sign for the Visitor Center soon after and we pulled into it. I spotted a coffee counter and made tracks toward it. Dad was pulling out brochures from a large display.

Sally suggested we walk around and stretch our legs. Pappa needed it most and he limped along with his cane. I walked in a wide circle around the periphery of the area. After I was out of hearing distance, I pulled out Tony's cell phone and called Becky. The situation was dire enough to commandeer his phone.

"What's going on?"

"Hi Meera! Can you believe it? They are saying Leo stole money from Charlie."

"Where is he right now?"

"They took him in for questioning. I think they will detain him today."

"Stan told me some woman claims she saw him. Who is this woman?"

"Must be a neighbor," Becky mused.

"Can you find out? Maybe talk to her if you can?"

"I'll see what I can do."

I didn't see a point in calling Stan. It was better to catch up with him at night. Tony had come up to where I was.

"Does he have a lawyer?"

I shrugged.

"We know nothing about him. Does he have any family, or someone he can call?"

"I thought he is on his own, Meera. Isn't that why Charlie took him in?"

"We don't know that for sure."

I completed the loop and sidled close to Motee Ba. I asked her about Leo's family. She gave me a weird look.

"Leo doesn't have anyone. I thought you knew that, Meera."

"I assumed that. But maybe he's just had a fight with his folks or something."

Motee Ba shook her head.

I felt the burden of responsibility weigh me down. How was I going to be of any help to Leo? I could think of no way other than calling Becky and asking her questions. Becky or Stan would have to be my conduits. I had to depend on them to find out the little things. Would Stan do my bidding, I wondered.

Pappa was looking around, waving his cane in the air, summoning everyone to the car. We got in and settled down. It was getting close to lunch.

"There's a small town off Route 66," Dad said, placing a finger on the map. "Tucumcari. Let's stop there for lunch."

"Where are we stopping tonight?" Jeet asked.

"Well, the plan was to go to Albuquerque," Dad said. "But your mother wants to visit Santa Fe."

He smiled at Sally and she smiled back.

"Won't that throw us off track?" I protested. "We are on a tight schedule here."

"Didn't you always want to visit Santa Fe?" Tony quirked his eyebrows. "It's supposed to be a ritzy joint."

I looked away, refusing to answer.

A few hills were beginning to appear on the horizon. Dad put in his CD again and cranked up the volume. It sounded like some old Bollywood songs from the 70s because Dad and Motee Ba started humming. After a while, Sally was humming too. I couldn't believe my ears.

When Sally went away all those years ago, she got flung around by a tornado. She forgot all about who she was. The doctor who found her took real good care of her. She ended up marrying him. Other than random dreams which made no sense to her, Sally had no idea who she was or where she came from until she found an old driver's license in her name and a letter written to her by her dear departed husband. She had set out to find her family and ended up in our lives.

Living with us had been good for Sally's memory. She remembered random things or events without realizing how. She didn't really remember her native language Gujarati, the one she had grown up with. Humming along with a Bollywood song was big. That meant another thread of Sally's memory had unraveled.

Dad finally caught up to what was happening. He jerked his head around, turning to stare at Sally. The car veered onto the shoulder and everyone shuddered as it went over the ruts.

"Watch out, boy!" Pappa yelled in fright.

Dad pulled over on the shoulder, jumped out and ran to the passenger side. He pulled open Sally's door and took her hands in his.

"Do you realize what you just did?"

She looked a bit uncertain.

"You were singing along with the song," Dad explained. "You remembered."

"I did?" Sally asked.

I guessed the humming had been spontaneous and she couldn't explain it.

Dad beamed at her. "Yes, you did. We saw this movie in 1976 back in Bombay, after we got engaged. You went around humming that song for days."

Bollywood movies are well known for their sound track. Sally was looking bewildered. It was as if a window had cracked open for an instant and shut with force.

"Stop badgering her, you fool," Pappa roared. "Get back on the road."

Dad couldn't stop grinning after that.

"I don't care what anyone says," he said. "This is progress."

We came across the town of Tucumcari.

"Look out for the murals," Jeet yelled, reading off a brochure. "There's a dinosaur museum and a Route 66 monument of some kind."

"Let's eat first," I groaned.

Dad drove around the town. The pueblo style houses with their flat roofs made a statement. We came across the murals and exclaimed over them. I had to get down and get photos. We drove Pappa crazy, posing around the murals forever.

I spotted a diner with a Route 66 sign over it and we filed in for lunch. They were serving an all day breakfast along with sandwiches and burgers. Everything had green chili on it.

The boys got burgers with lots of toppings, Tony going for the one with plenty of green chilies. Dad and Pappa got burritos and Sally got a big salad.

I went for a club sandwich which came with chilies! I gobbled the sandwich and said no to dessert. I sneaked out and dialed Stan's number. He answered immediately.

"I gathered you'd call, Meera."

"So what have you done?"

"We brought him in," Stan admitted. "He maintains he didn't take the money."

"Of course he didn't. Charlie Gibson was the goose that laid the golden egg. You think Leo would kill the goose for a measly egg?"

"I agree with you this time," Stan said.

This was like a historic moment. I sensed a but coming.

"It's this woman. She insists she saw him jump out of that window."

"What time did Charlie Gibson die? Did you find out?"

"Between 7 and 10 PM. The woman says she saw Leo jump out of the window around 7:30. So the time is about right."

"The last time we talked, you said this woman saw someone like Leo. How sure is she?"

"She's sounding very sure now. She insists it was Leo."

"How do you know she's not lying, Stan?"

"There's no reason to think that, Meera."

"What does Leo say? When did he leave for his trip?"

"Leo left some time after 7. He's not sure when. They had dinner at 6:30. He talked to Charlie about his trip. Charlie gave him some money, told him to take the car, and then Leo left."

"What about Leo's friends? If they can confirm he met them, he's in the clear, right?"

"He could have killed Charlie before going to meet his friends. So he goes to Ponca City, shoots the breeze with his friends, drives around and then comes back the next day."

"But why? Why would he do that? You don't have a motive."

Stan was quiet.

"Anna's making a lot of noise. She seems to have it in for the boy."

"Anna?"

"Anna Collins. She's the one who's claiming she saw Leo jumping out of the window."

A car honked beside me. Tony was driving and the seat next to him was empty. Everyone else was settled into their seats. Dad had a frown on his face. I hung up, promising to call back when I got a chance.

"Who were you talking to?" Dad asked.

"No one."

We stopped at a museum and exclaimed over the dinosaurs. Then it was time to move on.

"We should be there in a couple of hours," Dad said. "Have you picked a hotel out of those?"

Jeet and Dad looked through the brochures, trying to look for a midrange hotel. They narrowed down a couple of places close to the main shopping area. We stopped at a gas station just after Tony turned off I-40.

"We're leaving the old Route 66 now," Dad told Jeet. "But we'll be back on it after we reach Albuquerque."

It was past 4 PM by the time we checked into our hotel. Everyone voted for a short nap. I flung my shoes off and jumped onto the bed by the window. I couldn't dial Tony's phone fast enough.

Sylvie answered and I spent a few minutes assuring her all the Patels were doing great. I was getting impatient to talk to Becky.

"Who's Anna Collins? Have you ever met her?" I burst out as soon as I heard Becky grab the receiver.

"Let me ask Sylvie," Becky said.

I tried to hide my frustration. Sylvie came on the phone.

"What you want to know about Anna Collins, Meera?"

"Who is she?"

"You know her, Meera. Frumpy gal who works at the public library."

I didn't have much reason to visit the public library. The one at Pioneer Poly met all my needs. I tried to think back and remember who Sylvie was talking about. A frazzled, middle aged woman came to mind.

"Is she always going around with her head down?"

"That's the one," Sylvie agreed. "Stares at her feet most of the time. It's that thieving son of hers. She hardly ever looks anyone in the eye."

"You know her son?"

"Don Collins. A bad penny alright. Spends most of his time in prison."

"Where is he now?"

"I heard he just got off on parole. He sits around the house all day, drinking. Won't be long before he goes back in."

Becky grabbed the phone back from Sylvie.

"Why are you asking about Anna?"

"She's claiming she saw Leo jump out of the window. If she's so shy, why is she talking to the police all of a sudden?"

"Sylvie says she looks the other way even if she sees a cop car in the distance. It's because of her son."

"And this same woman is volunteering information?"

I heard Becky swear and say something she normally doesn't.

"Guess who just walked into the diner."

Chapter 7

It was almost dark when I woke up. The room was quiet and I was the only one in there. The phone rang. It was Jeet. Everyone was having tea in Motee Ba's room. I splashed some water on my face and stumbled out. I just followed the sound of the voices.

"I can hear you a mile away," I said, yawning my head off.

There was a tray of drinks sitting on a table. I smelled the coffee and picked one up gratefully.

"Who got this?"

"There's a café a block down the road," Tony said.

We are used to noshing on some heavy stuff in the evenings, so I was hungry. All kinds of snacks were spread out on a coffee table.

"We need to finish the *theplas* today," Motee Ba, said pointing to a stack of them.

A jar of mango relish stood next to them. There was a fresh box of *chevdo* Pappa was feasting over. A dozen *laddus* were beside them. These are fudgy balls made with flour, sugar and butter.

"Where are we going tonight?" I asked.

"The Plaza," Jeet said between mouthfuls of *laddu*.

"It's the central town square," Dad explained. "Let's just walk around and get a feel of the place. We are staying here tomorrow too so there's no rush."

"When are we going shopping?" I asked Motee Ba.

There was no way I was leaving here without some nice jewelry and spices.

Everyone got ready and we set off on foot. There were big sidewalks everywhere and people were roaming around. Santa Fe draws a lot of tourists year round. Pappa grumbled about the walk. Sally said something to him and he almost smiled.

We wandered along the shops in the Plaza, looking at what was on offer. There were shops selling local landscapes and pottery. Colored glass sculptures were on display in one. There was Native American jewelry and hand painted dinnerware. I didn't have enough money to buy everything I wanted.

The air was crisp and pleasant. I sat on a bench in the square, watching people. A troubadour broke into song just a few feet away from me. I was glad we were going to stay on for one whole day. The place was beginning to grow on me.

My phone rang, Tony's phone that is, and I rushed to answer it. Stan was on the line.

"We can't find Leo's friends, Meera."

"Why not?"

"They don't have phones. And Leo doesn't know anything else. Or he won't tell us. They are on Spring Break with no fixed plans. We can't track them down."

"Did you tell Leo how important it is that you talk to them?"

"We did."

I thought of what we had discussed before.

"Does he have a lawyer?"

"Not yet. The court will appoint one. Until then, he's staying in."

"What happens to Charlie Gibson's house? Does he have any relatives?"

Stan was quiet for a minute. I knew what that meant.

"I'll look into it. Hey, maybe your grandpa knows something. Why don't you ask him?"

"I never thought of that."

Stan hung up without saying much. Leo's fate was sealed and there was nothing Stan could do about it. Not based on the limited information he had.

Tony sat down next to me.

"Bad news?"

"Leo has no idea where those friends of his are. Or he won't tell."

Tony slapped his knee in frustration.

"What's your role in all this, Meera?"

My cheeks flamed. Was Tony ignoring the obvious?

"Look, when Pappa asked you to help, you didn't want to get involved. Now you're calling Becky and Stan every few hours, and exclaiming over anything they say."

"That's because what they are telling me is fantastic."

"That doesn't answer my question, Meera."

"Isn't it obvious? I want to help Leo get out of this mess. Prove he's innocent."

"What about being on vacation, enjoying the trip, and all that?"

I pursed my lips in thought.

"We are already on vacation. Look, I know I sounded like I didn't want any part of this before. Then I met Leo at the memorial service. I could sense how much Charlie's death affected him. He wasn't faking it, Tony. He was really grieving."

"So you want to prove Leo's innocent or you want to find Charlie's killer?"

"Aren't they the same things?"

"We don't know that right now," Tony said.

"Okay, I want to find out who harmed Charlie."

I gave Tony a look that screamed 'are you happy now?'

A slow smile spread across his face.

"You're finally getting on the right track."

I had no clue what he meant. Our time was up and I could see Dad waving at us from across the square. He was clutching plenty of fliers and brochures. Pappa was brandishing another cane.

"Got this at one of those shops," he crowed. "They are called Santa Fe sticks."

Pappa likes collecting walking sticks, although he uses only one at a time. He says he needs time to get used to them.

"There's a restaurant selling authentic New Mexican food just a block away," Dad said, waving his hand in a direction.

"I'm not walking all the way back to the hotel after dinner," Pappa protested.

Tony and I promised we would get the car and drive him back. That seemed to mollify him a bit. We walked into an adobo style building with a flat roof. The restaurant was bustling and we had to wait five minutes for a table.

"Should've reserved a table," Pappa glared at me.

These kinds of things fall under my purview.

I ordered chips with guacamole and queso for the table and asked the server to rush it. None of us deal well with hunger.

A huge platter arrived with small bowls of different kinds of salsa, and medium sized bowls filled to the brim with guacamole and queso. The chips were fresh and blue in color.

"What's this?" Pappa said uncertainly.

"These are blue corn chips," Sally explained. "They are a specialty of the region. Why don't you try one, Pappa?"

He shocked everyone by scooping up some guacamole with a chip. Apparently it met his approval, because he began crunching on them noisily. That gave me time to order a round of drinks for everyone. Tony wanted the chili burger and I wanted to try the enchiladas.

"Red or green?" the server asked when I placed the order.

"Excuse me?"

"The sauce," the server explained. "Do you want the red sauce or the green sauce?"

"Can I get both?"

In for a penny, I figured.

"Christmas," the server nodded and moved on to the rest of the order.

We were sitting in a courtyard. There were potted plants and urns full of flowers around us. Lights were strung overhead. The weather was cooling down but I was sure the food would warm us up soon enough.

We exclaimed over the food as the server set down our plates. Tony's burger came with a pile of green chilies on the side. My enchiladas were made with blue tortillas, a first for me. There was a thick layer of Monterey Jack cheese and the red and green sauces. A generous serving of pinto beans and spicy rice was served with the enchiladas. Dad's burrito had red sauce ladled over it, along with cheese. Smothered, the server had called it. Sally told us that's how they served burritos in New Mexico.

Sally piled chilies on her burger and bit into it. She closed her eyes in pleasure.

"This is one of the best burgers in the world," she exclaimed.

I realized she had come there before, probably with her other husband.

We walked over to a place selling chocolate gelato for dessert. Tony and I went back to the hotel to get the car while everyone else waited. I had expected to feel drowsy after the heavy dinner but I was feeling energized.

"You want me to be methodical," I told Tony as we turned a

corner.

"Begin at the beginning," he said. "Focus on the truth. Don't start with a theory and try to fit the facts to it."

"We don't have a white board with us."

"So what, Meera? Use pen and paper. We need a logical and systematic approach. Don't you agree?"

A plan began to take shape in my mind and I felt better. I punched Tony's arm, and he punched me back. We had almost worked off dinner by the time we reached the hotel. I was ready for the gelato.

Jeet suggested a card game when we got back but the grownups were asleep on their feet.

"We're going into the mountains tomorrow," Dad smiled, waving some brochures. "It's going to be awesome."

Jeet started dealing cards as soon as we entered our room. I found a small notepad the hotel had provided and began making a list.

"Pay attention, Meera!" Jeet pouted when I missed my turn the third time. "What're you writing anyway?"

He snatched the pad away from me and his eyes grew wide.

"Dad won't like this. You promised to stay away from all this."

"I did no such thing," I scoffed. "Go to bed, little brother."

"Aren't you scared, Meera?" Jeet wondered. "What if someone tries to harm you?"

The thought had crossed my mind. I remembered the close call I had last time. I had got away lightly.

"We're far away from the scene of the crime," I pointed out. "And I'm not alone."

Jeet gave me a queer look and pulled the covers over his head.

Tony had picked up the notepad and he was reading through it.

"Pappa might be able to answer some of these questions. And so can Charlie's housekeeper."

"We need to make a list of the people Charlie interacted with. That might give us an idea about the possible motive."

Tony started writing down names. Leo and the housekeeper were the only people Charlie Gibson dealt with on a regular basis. Then there were people like Sylvie, his neighbors, and people at the bank or library. I would start by talking to Pappa.

"Do you think Pappa's still up?" I asked Tony.

"Better wait until morning."

I called Becky and I told her all about Santa Fe.

"I want to talk to this Audrey Jones."

"Charlie's housekeeper?" Becky asked. "She rarely comes in here."

"If I give you a list of questions, can you go and talk to her?"

Becky wasn't too confident about the job. Talking to Audrey on the phone would cost a fortune. Was that my only option?

"Do you have your questions ready?" Becky relented.

"Well, not exactly. It's just some background on Charlie, you know. What was he like. Who he met on a regular basis, how he got along with his neighbors, was there something different about him last week…"

"I can't remember all that!"

"It's the same stuff we asked Mary Beth or Pamela."

I was referring to people we had come across earlier that year while solving the other two cases.

"Do you think this will get Leo out of jail?"

"I'm doing this to find out who murdered Charlie. If Leo's innocent, he'll be fine."

Chapter 8

I felt like sleeping in the next day since we were just spending time in Santa Fe. The loud banging on the door killed any chance of that.

"We don't want housekeeping!" Tony yelled in a voice heavy with sleep.

"Didn't you hang the Do Not Disturb sign on the door?" I hissed.

"Housekeeping doesn't come knocking at 6 AM," Jeet scoffed at us.

The banging had continued all this time. The phone trilled next and I snatched it up.

"Yeah?" I said, annoyed.

"Be ready in an hour," Motee Ba commanded. "Why aren't you letting your Dad in?"

"That's Dad at the door? What's the rush?"

Jeet had opened the door by then and Dad burst in.

"Time to wake up," he said cheerfully. "We hit the trail in an hour."

Three blank faces stared at him. Dad sighed and tapped his watch.

"One hour. Outside!"

He turned around and slammed the door on his way out, jarring my senses.

"I thought this was a rest day," Jeet complained. "What's with him, anyway?"

The hotel offered a Continental breakfast with the usual cereal and baked goods. Dad had picked out a local café for us.

"Huevos Rancheros!" he announced, licking his lips. "You can't come to Santa Fe and not try the huevos rancheros, right?"

He looked at Sally for approval and she gave him a wide smile. Everyone got the same order. Tony got some carne asada steak to go with his breakfast. I plunged my fork into the gooey beans, cheese and eggs on a base of fried tortillas. It was all smothered in red sauce. It was hard to tell where the tortillas ended and the beans and cheese started. It all came together in one perfect heavenly bite.

Sally and Motee Ba ordered hot chocolate and it was dark, thick and creamy, laced with plenty of cinnamon. I stuck to my coffee.

Dad sprang up and herded us to the car the moment we had finished eating.

"What's the rush?" I cribbed. "Aren't we supposed to take it easy on vacation?"

"The early bird gets the worm," he said cryptically, and laughed.

We pulled up in front of a large building a few minutes later. A sign announced it to be the Santa Fe Farmer's Market. A motley group of old guys was playing some music at one side. Farmers and artisans were selling their wares from impromptu stands and tables. There were chilies of all colors. Green chilies ranged from pale yellow to the darkest green. Bottles of fresh made green chili salsa were on display everywhere. Pies and sopapillas were being sold in one corner, perfuming the air with the scent of fried pastry. A lady was selling fresh made tortillas and another counter sold chili seasonings and herbs.

Dad bought a bunch of flowers from a stand and gave them to Sally with a flourish. She turned around, pretending to sniff them, trying to hide her blush. My hand rose spontaneously to make a gagging motion. Motee Ba struck it down.

I grabbed her arm and started walking in the other direction. An old lady offered us samples of goat cheese, and I licked the salty, sharp cheese off my fingers. I almost forgot what I wanted to tell my grandma.

We had come up to a farmer selling dried red chilies. Garlands of red chilies hung from pegs. There were smaller bunches on the table.

"We're so getting these!" I exclaimed.

"Are these used in the red sauce they make over here?" I asked the middle aged man selling them.

He nodded his head. "These are the Hatch chilies the area is famous for. You can also get the fresh green ones."

I got a few bundles of the dry red chili to take home with us. I couldn't resist some of the fresh green chili. I didn't know how we were going to eat them. Sally appeared with a large bag full of stuff. Dad followed with another bag.

"I am going to find out what happened to Charlie," I told Motee Ba before the others caught up with us.

She clutched my arm, looking grateful. "Wait till I tell your Pappa."

"I need to talk to him, Motee Ba. Ask him about Charlie."

"You can do it today, any time you get a chance. Just let me talk to him first."

"What about Dad?" I asked, tipping my head toward the car.

He was busy helping Sally stash the new purchases in the back of the car. Dad and Jeet were pushing back our luggage while Sally found space for the farmer's market purchases.

"You can't talk in the car," Motee Ba said, catching on. "We'll think of something. And we can talk in our room later tonight."

Pappa called out to us just then, tapping his cane. He was getting impatient. Everyone got in and Dad took the wheel.

"We are taking the high road," he proclaimed.

All pairs of eyes stared at him.

"No, really, we are taking the high road to Taos. But we have to make a pit stop first."

He stopped outside a super market and signaled Tony to follow him. Jeet followed them inside.

"So you're going to help me get justice for my friend?" Pappa asked me.

Motee Ba must have managed to whisper something to him. I looked at Sally.

"Your mother won't say anything, Meera."

I gave Motee Ba a look. She must have missed all those secret looks flying between Dad and Sally. I wasn't so sure she wouldn't tattle against me. But I didn't have much of a choice.

"I want to get some background on Charlie. When can we talk, Pappa?"

Dad and the boys came back lugging more bags. We had to place these by our feet. Pappa whispered something in my ear and I nodded. I picked up one of Dad's brochures and skimmed through them.

"Are we going to these waterfalls?" I asked.

"That's our first stop," Dad said eagerly. "The Nambe pueblo. We are going to the base of the Sangre De Cristo mountains."

He looked at Jeet. "You up for a little hike?"

"What about Pappa?" I asked. "Can he manage this trail?"

Pappa declared he wasn't up to any strenuous activity.

"I've always wanted to see a pueblo," Motee Ba told him. "It says the trail is less than a quarter mile."

"But I don't want to go Hansa!" Pappa said with some force.

"I can stay with Pappa," I said. "You can all go ahead."

"You want to miss this after coming all the way here?" Dad exclaimed.

I shrugged.

Truth be told, someone would have to keep Pappa company whenever we did something like this. We would all have to take turns.

"I won't do it every time," I warned.

I mentally congratulated myself on being smart. We reached the pueblo and everyone got down.

"You can stay in sight of the car and look around," Dad mused. "Pappa should be okay with that."

"I'm fine, Dad," I said, trying to put some sass in my voice.

Dad shrugged and they set off to see the waterfall.

I stood on the ground with the car door open, letting fresh air in. Pappa wanted a drink. I handed him one and placed a shawl on his knees.

"Fire away, Meera," he said, sipping his juice.

"What can you tell me about Charlie?"

"He was my friend. But he kept everyone at a distance."

"Did he argue with people a lot?"

"Not exactly."

Pappa paused, giving it some thought.

"He was polite enough, but there was something missing. As if he was being forced to do something."

"You mean like blackmail?"

"No, Meera," Pappa sighed. "As if his heart wasn't in it."

"So he was cold, you mean."

Pappa nodded uncertainly.

"That's why we were all surprised when he brought that boy home."

"Leo? Where did he meet him? Is he a distant relation?"

"Not as far as I know. Charlie said he was getting on. And he wanted to share whatever he had with someone who needed it."

"So what, he just picked the first random kid he came across?"

"He didn't want to talk about it," Pappa explained. "He made it very clear. Anything about Leo was off limits."

"But why?"

"How should I know?" Pappa asked.

"Was he rich?"

"He lived well. But he wasn't rolling in money."

"So you don't think anyone would kill him for money?"

Pappa looked disturbed.

"I have seen people bludgeoned to death for a few shillings, Meera. Need is relative. Your coffee money can feed a poor family in India for a month."

This is one of Pappa's pet theories. He really frowns upon the money I spend in coffee shops. I forced myself to ignore it. It was more important to focus on the job at hand.

"What about Charlie's family? Did he have any kids?"

"His wife died before we came to Swan Creek," Pappa said. "They didn't have children."

"Who's getting his things now that he's gone? Did he ever talk about a will?"

"Charlie believed in being prepared. Everything was to be sold and the proceeds were to be donated to his favorite charity. But lately…"

Pappa paused to take a sip of his juice. He sucked the straw until there was a gurgling sound and the box crumpled.

"Got any more of this?"

"You can drink water if you're still thirsty, Pappa."

His lip curled into an expression of disgust. I could hear Jeet and Tony talking. It sounded like they were coming back.

"Lately?" I reminded Pappa.

"He was talking of changing it. I think he wanted to provide for the boy."

"Did he actually say that?"

"He asked me what was better – giving money to an organization and not knowing how it would be used, or giving it to someone you knew who actually needed it."

It did sound like Charlie was having second thoughts.

"Did he end up changing this will of his?"

"Your guess is as good as mine, Meera."

There was a shout and I turned to see my family walk across, wide smiles lighting their faces.

"We'll talk later," I whispered and signaled Pappa to be quiet.

"What a sight, eh?" Dad exclaimed. "You missed it, Meera. It was beautiful. Ask your mother."

Sally smiled.

I had no intention of asking her anything. I ignored Dad and turned toward the boys.

"Why are you wet?"

"We took a different trail," Jeet explained. "It climbed down right up to the falls. The water's too cold to go in though."

I couldn't hide my disappointment. Tony was quick to pick up on it.

"Do you want to go down there, Meera?"

"Nah! I'm fine. There's plenty more to see today."

"You can drive now, Tony," Dad said, tossing the keys to him.

"Shotgun!" Jeet cried and jumped into the front seat before I could say anything.

Dad and Sally climbed into the back, and I squeezed in next to Motee Ba.

"Where to?" Tony asked.

"Get onto 503," Dad directed Tony.

He handed over the map to Jeet.

"It's just 10 miles to the next stop. Let's see if you can get us there."

"El Pocito," Sally mumbled, crossing herself.

My mouth fell open. What business did Sally have, making the sign of the cross?

Motee Ba took my hand in hers and shook her head. It was code for sucking it up. I took my mind off what was happening in the back seat and started analyzing what Pappa had told me.

Chapter 9

El Santuario De Chimayo was a small adobe church unlike any I had seen before. The earth inside this church is famous for its healing powers. We stared at letters and testimonials displayed in a prayer room, talking about the miracles they had experienced by coming there. Another room had a small well with this earth. Sally packed some of it in a Ziploc bag.

"Having your mother back with us is nothing short of a miracle," Motee Ba said with tears in her eyes.

We visited some weaving shops and admired the rugs and blankets on offer. I got a bag of the local chilies from a mercantile. We were ready to drive on to our next stop.

The road climbed into the mountains as we left the verdant valley behind. We drove through villages resplendent with Spanish architecture and culture. Mountains lined the horizon, their peaks covered with snow.

"I'm hungry," Jeet said suddenly, breaking the silence.

Everyone wanted to eat something. Sally passed a bag to Motee Ba.

"What are we doing for lunch?" Pappa asked.

"It's barely noon," Dad snorted. "I have big plans for lunch, Pappa. It's a surprise."

Motee Ba passed out tamales along with plastic spoons. Sally handed out some fruit. Tony pulled over to the side and we gave some serious attention to the food. We reached the town of Taos and saw the sights. Dad was getting excited. He took the wheel and we headed into a forest.

"Are we going camping?" Jeet asked.

Pappa opened his mouth to protest. At his age, he doesn't like to rough it.

"No, we're just having lunch."

Dad drove a few miles and entered a campground. He drove around until he found the perfect spot. All the shopping from that morning began to make sense. I jumped down and helped Pappa and Motee Ba out of the car. Everyone stretched and yawned. The drive from the last stop had been little more than an hour, but I was glad to be out in the fresh air.

The weather was pleasant, somewhere in the 60s. There was plenty of verdant forest around us. A stream gurgled past the campsite and there was a fire pit and a grill. There was a primitive toilet somewhere in the distance. I would rather do my business in the woods.

"This is the Rio Fernando," Dad said, reading from the brochure.

"Put that away now," Pappa ordered. "It's past my lunch time."

We cleaned up a big stone bench and Sally and Motee Ba settled down. They began to unload a ton of bags. Dad and the boys wanted to walk around and explore. They looked at me beseechingly.

"You know how to get the grill going, Meera."

"No problem, Dad!" I waved them off.

I turned around and stared at the bounty on the picnic table. There was a heap of tomatoes, avocados and limes. Sally was peeling garlic. Motee Ba was still pulling out goodies. There was a bottle of seasoning and a jar of green chili sauce. I shook my head and started cleaning the grill.

"Let's grill some chicken and corn," Motee Ba suggested, pointing to the stuff. "Any other ideas?"

"We can make a salad with the tomatoes and avocados," I nodded. "And a chili honey marinade for the corn."

Sally smiled and began chopping tomatoes. I sprinkled salt and chili on the chicken and borrowed the knife to chop some garlic.

"You said you were supposed to meet Charlie for lunch that day."

I looked up at Pappa. He was pacing the area, tapping his cane, muttering something about having to go hungry.

"Yes, on Wednesday."

"Did he want to talk about something?"

"We met for lunch once a month. The first Wednesday was reserved for me."

"What do you mean?"

"Charlie was very particular about his schedule. He had days set aside for doing chores. Wednesday was his day to socialize – meet friends for lunch."

"So you always met on the first Wednesday of the month?"

"Ever since I've known him," Pappa nodded. "Unless something important came up or one of us was ill."

Had someone wanted to prevent Charlie from meeting Pappa? My mind was working fast as I cleaned the fire pit and put the coals in. I got the fire going and waited for the grill to heat up. Sally started placing the chicken on the grill. I placed the corn on the other end. I fixed a plate for Pappa as soon as the first piece of chicken was done.

"This is good," he said, smacking his lips, licking his fingers.

The green chili sauce and honey made the corn pop. We had some salty goat's cheese from the farmer's market and I crumbled it on the corn. Cubes of Queso Fresco went into the tomato and avocados.

"What did he do on Tuesday?" I asked Pappa.

"Tuesday was for Sylvie and her meatloaf. He never missed it."

"What else did he do? He must have done something other than having lunch."

Pappa didn't know about that.

"Sylvie or Jon might know," Motee Ba said. "Maybe Charlie mentioned something while having lunch."

"He wasn't one for small talk," Pappa warned.

I mentally filed it away as one of the questions I had for Sylvie.

Dad and the boys came back hungry and there was a sudden rush for the food. I flipped chicken while eating from my own plate, polishing off every little bite. Sally produced some sopapillas and we doused them with the natural honey from the market. The hungriest tummy was finally full and we grew quiet, taking in the surroundings. Although the place was just off the highway, there was a tranquil atmosphere all around. We were at a high elevation and the sky seemed a bit lower. I felt I could almost touch the fluffy white clouds.

Tony pulled me to my feet to show me a small wooden bridge that spanned the rivulet. Jeet and Dad began clearing up. We drove straight back to Santa Fe after that, although we stopped to take plenty of pictures at scenic spots along the way.

The sun was setting by the time we got back to our hotel. We agreed to meet for dinner at 8. I freshened up and talked Tony into going for a walk near the Plaza. I still hadn't got a single turquoise ornament and I meant to remedy that.

"Did you manage to talk to Pappa at all?" Tony asked as we set out.

"Charlie didn't want to talk about Leo's background. But he wanted to change his will and leave something to Leo."

Tony's eyes widened.

"Pappa doesn't think Charlie was rich though. He got by."

"Rich or poor is relative, Meera."

"That's just what Pappa said. And he said Charlie was a cold fish."

"So someone might have had a grudge against him."

"For what, Tony?"

He shrugged.

We wandered around and met the family. Dinner was another round of tasty local food. I couldn't get enough of the chile rellenos, a large poblano pepper stuffed full of cheese, smothered in an earthy red sauce, served with the ever present beans and rice.

I called Becky from the room. She wanted to know what we had done all day. I finally steered her to the matter at hand.

"So? Did you talk to Charlie's housekeeper?"

"Her name is Audrey Jones," Becky supplied. "She came into the diner today for coffee. Sylvie gave her pie on the house."

I was getting impatient.

"She was shy at first – doesn't go out much. But she was on a roll once she started talking."

"Did you ask her the questions like I told you?"

"I couldn't get a word in," Becky said. "But she did talk about Charlie."

I was eager to learn what this housekeeper had to talk about. Becky didn't need much prompting.

"She's worked for Charlie for almost 20 years, since his wife passed. Charlie never gave her a compliment. Not even once in all these years. But he paid her on time, and gave her a raise every year."

"So she didn't have anything to complain about then."

"She seemed a bit miffed, I don't know why. He never sat around talking with her it seems. Just said what was necessary and that was it. She has a bad knee. I guess he didn't pay attention when she talked about her aches and pains."

"What did she do for him, exactly?"

"Cleaned the house, did laundry and cooked."

"So she went there every day?"

"Twice a day every day with not a single day off. She got half a day off on Christmas and Thanksgiving but she had to cook his meal first."

"Sounds like a tyrant alright."

"Could've been worse," Becky said philosophically. "Sylvie said Audrey's not that great a worker. She barely does her job and she's a bad cook."

"Did Charlie say that?"

"I don't think so. Sylvie just knows."

Sylvie is firmly tuned into the Swan Creek grapevine. If you want to get the skinny on someone, she's your guy.

"Why did Charlie Gibson keep her on then?"

"I don't know that, Meera," Becky yawned, sounding bored.

"You don't think they …"

I paused, but Becky got the idea.

"Ewww, no, I don't think so. And she's married."

"When has that ever stopped anyone from straying?"

"You're going off track, Meera."

"What else did she say? Anything about what Charlie was doing that day?"

"Charlie always came to the diner on Tuesdays. So she didn't make lunch that day. And dinner was light, just a sandwich."

"What about Leo? Did he also come to the diner every Tuesday?"

"I don't remember seeing him."

"So what did Leo do when Charlie went out for lunch?" I remembered he went out for lunch on Wednesdays too.

"Ate leftovers?" Becky asked. "You'll have to ask him about it."

Did Leo care what he ate for lunch? I doubt he had the money to buy himself a burger.

"Did she make their dinner that last Tuesday? When did she leave? Ask her anything you can about what Charlie did that day."

"She's coming here tomorrow. I'll try to talk to her."

Tony and I discussed what Becky had said.

"I remember Mom wanted some help with the house. She talked to this woman, I think."

I made Tony call Aunt Reema right then. We needed to catch up with her anyway.

"You don't know what you're missing!" I exclaimed. "The food here is just amazing. And the view changes every hour."

Tony finally got around to asking her about Audrey Jones.

"Oh yeah! She comes around once a week. Helps me with some dusting. Not that good at her job, though. She charges by the hour and watches TV most of the time."

"Why do you keep her on then?" Tony asked his mother.

"I just haven't got around to finding someone else."

We chatted with Aunt Reema some more and hung up.

"So Audrey Jones likes to talk, and she's lazy. And she's a bad cook."

"None of that is a crime," Tony observed.

"No, it isn't," I agreed.

"Want to call Stan?" Tony asked.

"I'm too tired. He'll call if anything changes."

I wrote something down on the notepad.

"Did you make any progress today?" Tony asked.

"I'm still finding pieces of the puzzle. There's a lot to do before I start piecing it together."

Chapter 10

We woke up without much fuss the next morning. It was a travel day and I was looking forward to napping in the car. Dad had other plans.

"You climb about 4000 feet in just 15 minutes," he was telling Motee Ba enthusiastically.

"I'm not getting into any death trap," Pappa declared. "I'm getting tired of this walking around."

"I will stay back with you," Motee Ba assured him.

"Isn't this our day on the road?" I asked Dad.

"It is, Meera. But we're passing through Albuquerque. Your mother says …"

He turned to Sally and patted her on the shoulder.

"Tell them!"

Sally looked at us and smiled.

"The Sandia Mountains are beautiful. You'll love the cable car."

"I thought you can see these Sandia Mountains from anywhere in the city," Jeet said, reading some brochure.

"We are going to the top," Dad cried, "almost 2 miles high."

We were having breakfast at a small café in Santa Fe. Dad had taken the initiative and ordered breakfast burritos for everyone. They came loaded with eggs, potatoes, cheese and beans, smothered in a green chili sauce with more cheese on top.

Everyone got in and Sally took the wheel. Dad urged me to ride shotgun with her. I found out why soon enough as a bunch of snores filled the car. Sally was her usual quiet self and I wasn't feeling too kindly toward her. I had no idea why. We made good time and entered Albuquerque within an hour. It was the morning rush hour and an eight lane road yawned ahead of us.

Cars whizzed past, passing each other with barely enough room.

I sucked in a breath. I felt like a country bumpkin.

Sally maneuvered the car skillfully without batting an eyelid.

"Your mother's used to the traffic here," Dad said, as if answering a question. "She comes here a lot."

"Why do you come here?" I asked Sally suspiciously.

She gave a brief smile without taking her eyes off the road.

"Your mother lived in this area before moving to California," Dad informed me. "She knows people in the area."

"We're not going to meet any people, are we?" I said in disgust.

"Not this time," Dad said.

Sally gave me one more smile. This one probably meant 'Don't worry.' She hardly ever says anything but there is a pattern to her smiles. I was developing an uncanny ability of translating her smiles into words.

"Where are we?" Pappa asked hoarsely.

He had just woken up from a deep sleep.

"Are those the Sandia mountains, Mom?" Jeet asked, pointing to a mountain range lining the horizon.

Sally smiled at him in the rearview mirror and nodded. We pulled up in a parking lot and got in line to get the tickets.

"Maybe I should wait with Pappa," I said.

"No need," Dad said firmly. "Ba's keeping him company. You missed the waterfalls yesterday."

In the end, I was glad I got into the cable car. It whisked us up and we slowly progressed to the top of the mountain. The view expanded as we rose higher and soon we were staring down at the treetops. I zipped up my jacket as we got off the car at the top. There was a café and some people were heading off toward the ski slopes. Plenty of snow lined the mountain side. We laughed with sheer pleasure and took pictures.

Dad made me take a picture of him and Sally standing below the elevation sign. I had to comply.

We took the car down and walked toward Pappa and Motee Ba. Pappa was impatient, tapping his cane and grumbling.

"There's a fabulous walking trail that goes through the center of town…" Dad began.

"Enough!" Pappa roared. "We are getting back on the road now."

Sally put a hand on Dad's arm.

"Okay, okay. How about we pack some lunch? That way, we can just eat on the way without stopping anywhere."

"Now you're talking sense," Pappa said, struggling to his feet.

Dad and Tony went into a burger place to order lunch. Luckily there was a crafts store next to the burger place. I went in and got some supplies. I had an idea about how I was going to use them.

I stashed the bags under a seat before Dad could see them.

"Charlie Gibson never came to our house, did he?" I asked Motee Ba.

Most of Pappa's friends come over for tea or a meal quite often. Then there is the annual Diwali party we throw. Almost everyone we know is invited.

"We sent him an invite every time we had a party. He never showed up."

Charlie Gibson was eccentric alright. I was beginning to wonder how many people he had unknowingly hurt by his behavior.

Dad and Tony came back with two giant bags bursting with food. We could smell the steaming meat and fries.

"Barely 11:30," Dad said, looking at his watch. "We can stop in an hour."

Sally pulled out the car and we merged onto I-40 W once again.

"Back on Route 66," Dad called out.

Dad cranked up the volume and began singing along with his CD.

"Is this the only music we are listening to on this trip?" I bristled.

Dad ignored me. Sally was humming along with him. Dad looked totally besotted, sort of like Jeet does when he has a new girl friend. I must have been staring at them for a long time.

Tony elbowed me and cleared his throat.

"You're drooling."

Motee Ba handed me a tissue.

"Your mother has a good voice," she said, pouring oil on troubled waters.

"Like a nightingale," Pappa said, bobbing his head. "What was that song she always sang at parties, Hansa?"

They argued over it for some time. Sally started humming a tune. Dad switched the CD off and let her sing.

"That's the one," Pappa said.

Dad clapped his hands and Sally looked happy. I sulked, keeping my head firmly turned toward the window.

We came upon a good rest area and stopped for lunch. We made quick work of the chili burgers and fries. Jeet pulled out some cold drinks from a vending machine.

I signaled Tony and we got up to stretch our legs. I took his phone and called the diner. Sylvie answered. I assured her everyone was doing fine and everyone missed them.

"Did Charlie ever mention what he did before coming to you on Tuesdays?" I asked her.

"Well, he wasn't a big talker," Sylvie mused. "Your grandpa will tell you that."

I hoped Sylvie would get to the point soon. Tony was going to end up with a big cell phone bill this month.

"I think he went to the library before coming to our place," Sylvie said. "He always had a stack of books with him."

"Maybe he was planning to return them?" I spoke out loud.

"I don't think so. He used to pick up one book from the pile and start reading it while he had his meal here."

"Did he ever get something to go?"

"Never!" Sylvie said. "I offered him a slice of pie once but he said no. He didn't want to overindulge after the meatloaf."

"So he didn't get an extra helping or something to take home?"

"Our portions are generous, Meera. You know that! Keep a man going all day."

I knew Sylvie wasn't stingy with her portions. I had wondered if Charlie took anything home for Leo.

"Did he say anything particular that day?"

I could imagine Sylvie shaking her head from side to side.

"Said Thank You when I placed his plate on the table, remarked on the weather…that's about all he ever said."

"Did he look worried, or angry? Different from usual?"

"Can't say he did, Meera. Came in at 12:30 like always, polished off his plate and left."

"What's Becky up to?"

"She had to deliver an order. She said she might drive by Charlie Gibson's house and talk to his neighbor."

I felt a burst of excitement. "She did? Can you ask her to call me tonight please?"

"Sure, baby," Sylvie laughed. "She'll do that anyway."

I thought of something.

"Becky told me you said Audrey Jones wasn't that good at her job?"

"She's lazy. That's what she is."

"Why did Charlie keep her on all these years?"

"Now I never thought of that," Sylvie mused. "Maybe no one else wanted to work for him."

"She works for Aunt Reema too," I volunteered. "Sits around watching TV most of the time."

"Audrey works for Reema?" Sylvie asked, surprised. "Are you sure?"

"Tony and I just talked to her yesterday. Why?"

"Charlie had a condition. Audrey wasn't allowed to work for anyone else."

"But why?"

"He could be whimsical, Meera. Maids have a tendency to gossip. He didn't want anyone talking about him."

"Was there something to talk about?" I raised an eyebrow, then realized Sylvie couldn't see it.

"Maybe he just liked his privacy. If you ask me, Charlie Gibson was the most boring person in Swan Creek. I have never seen him do anything spontaneous."

"Why did Audrey agree to this exclusive condition? She can't have made enough working for Charlie alone?"

"He gave her a raise every year," Sylvie said. "Obviously, she was taking on other jobs though."

"What do you think Charlie would do if he found out?"

"Fire her!" Sylvie was confident. "He didn't tolerate any

nonsense."

Had Audrey got into a fight with Charlie over her job?

"Isn't she coming to the diner today?" I asked Sylvie.

"That's what she said. She has a lot of time on her hands now. And some extra cash to burn, looks like."

"Do you think she stole the money?"

Sylvie grunted.

"If she was light fingered, she wouldn't have lasted in that job."

Sylvie had to take care of the diner customers and Tony was giving me the evil eye. I hung up, and tried to look innocent.

"Why are you using up my daytime minutes, Meera?"

"Relax! I'll help you with your bill this time."

"You're paying the whole darn thing, Meera!"

I rolled my eyes and we walked back to the car. Dad and Sally were settled in the back seat.

"When can I drive?" Jeet asked.

"Maybe tomorrow?" I said.

Tony wanted to drive and I was okay with that. I settled into the front seat and popped in a CD of my choice. We were in for a 4-5 hour drive.

"Where to?" Tony asked.

"Keep going west on I-40," Dad called out.

The folks in the back started playing 20 Questions. Tony put the car on Cruise and looked at me. We had talked about taking this trip for a long time. I felt a sudden urge to hold his hand. Then I curbed myself. Tony's pupils widened and he gave me a sly smile. I looked away, trying to hide my blush.

He reads my mind every time.

Chapter 11

Pappa wanted a break. That set the others off. We had just entered the state of Arizona. Jeet had made us stop near the Welcome to Arizona sign for a quick photo.

"We need to get these photos printed," I said, waving the camera in the air.

There weren't too many people at the rest area and the restrooms were clean. I did my business and stood in front of the mirror, straightening my hair. Something caught my eye. It was too small to be graffiti. I peered closer and tried to make sense out of the drawing. Why would someone doodle on a crumbling wall in a yucky restroom in the middle of nowhere?

I looked around, looking for any more drawings. I didn't find any. Must be some kid, I thought and stepped out. Another doodle stared me in the face. This one was drawn on a wooden pillar with what seemed like chalk. I made a mental note to look it up in the brochures Jeet had picked up. Maybe it was something local to Arizona.

The desert landscape was sparsely populated. I was eager to spot the giant cactuses that shot up 20-30 feet high. The mood in the car was upbeat. Dad took advantage of it and slid a brochure in front of Pappa.

"Now what? No stops, Andy!"

"It's on the way, Pappa. Please!"

He sounded like a child.

Pappa grunted something unintelligible and gave a slight nod.

"Take the next exit Meera!" Dad crowed.

I turned just in time, barely enough to read the sign announcing the Meteor Crater.

"30 minutes tops," Pappa ordered.

"You can get down here, Pappa," Dad said. "This is a geological marvel."

In Jeet's words, it was just one big giant hole in the ground.

A paved path ran around the periphery of the crater. People were walking along it, doing a loop.

"We don't have enough time to walk around," Dad said wistfully.

There was a small museum with photos and stuff about meteors.

"Just imagine. A giant ball of fire came out of the sky and crashed here."

Dad was reading the history of the crater, trying to get everyone to feel his excitement. Tony and I skimmed through the displays and I dragged him out on the pretext of checking out the trail.

"Don't go too far," Dad warned. "We're done here."

The family had already started going toward the car. We walked at a brisk pace until they were out of hearing range.

"Did Sylvie say something?"

I shook my head.

"All I gathered is Charlie Gibson probably went to the library every Tuesday morning. And he didn't believe in small talk or compliments."

"Hmm…" Tony said.

"Hey, did you notice any small doodles in that rest area we stopped at?"

"You mean like graffiti?"

"Sort of, but not very large. Maybe an inch by inch in size?"

"Not really."

We went back to the car and I started driving.

"We should be there in an hour or so," Dad said, trying to mollify Pappa.

We were stopping in the famous town of Williams, Arizona, gateway to the Grand Canyon. We would be there for two nights before heading west again. I was determined to talk to Becky and Stan as much as I could over these two days.

The sun was low on the horizon when I pulled into the hotel's parking lot. The sky was ablaze in shades of orange and red. It was a desert sunset unlike any. If we were lucky, we would be able to watch the sun set over the canyon tomorrow. I waited until everyone got down and all the bags were unloaded. Then I turned the key in the ignition.

"Where are you off to now, Meera?" Motee Ba said sharply.

"Just dropping off these photos."

I had spotted a sign for one hour prints and I wasn't going to miss the chance. Tony and I were back soon enough. We spotted the gang having coffee in the hotel's restaurant. They waved us over.

"Can you believe it?" Pappa said with awe. "We are at the Grand Canyon."

My grandparents had talked about visiting many times. But they had never had the opportunity. My aunt and uncle had made a few trips here and they had wanted to take Pappa and Motee Ba along. But my grandmother had always stayed back home, loathe to hand us over to some baby sitter.

Sally's absence had shaped our life in certain ways so far. I sensed her presence was going to shape our future too. Dad and Jeet stayed at the table, pouring over a stack of brochures. I was fine with whatever plan they came up with for the next day.

I went to my room, or rather, our room, the one I shared with the boys. A long hot shower sounded good to me. I felt I could tackle whatever Becky had in store for me after that.

Tony and Jeet were lounging on their beds, watching a movie on the TV.

"We're meeting for dinner at 8," Jeet told me. "The restaurant closes at 8:30."

Thankfully, Dad had decided to eat at the hotel restaurant. That didn't leave much time for what I had in mind. I threw the car keys to Tony and headed toward the door.

"Do we have to go now?" he grumbled.

"Aren't you eager to see the photos?"

"I can drive you," Jeet said hopefully.

"Thanks, buddy!" I said without turning back. "But I got this."

Tony and I got back in half an hour. Luckily, there was still time for dinner. There were over a hundred photos. I split them up in three piles and we began rifling through them.

"Mom and Dad look hot together," Jeet exclaimed.

He was looking at the photo I took at the top of the mountain. I ignored him. Something clicked in my mind for a nanosecond. But then I couldn't remember what it was.

Motee Ba knocked on our door. It was time for dinner.

I ordered Chicken Parmesan, one of my favorite meals. It seemed almost simple after all the spicy stuff we had eaten in New Mexico. It was our fourth day on the road and everyone was looking tired.

"No staying up late tonight," Dad warned. "Tomorrow's going to be hectic."

Dad's eyes bore into me as he said this. I nodded. I had other plans.

I called Becky the moment we got back to the room. I rushed through what we had done that day, playing it down. I could sense Becky's mood going downhill as I talked about all the fun I was having without her.

"Did you drive by Charlie's house?" I asked finally.

Becky started explaining where she had gone for her delivery, who she had met and all that. I had to steer her back to the point.

"Alright, Meera. I'm getting to it."

"Did you meet this Anna?"

"I wasn't sure where she lives," Becky began. "I parked in Charlie's driveway. You know how his house is in a cul de sac."

"Yeah."

"I walked around a bit. I was hoping someone would come out of their house."

"And did they?"

"I saw the curtains move in one house. But no one came out."

"What about Anna?"

"Well, I started reading the mailboxes and spotted one with Collins written on it. I knocked on the door."

I held my breath.

"A man yelled from inside," Becky said. "Asked me to go away."

"So you left?" I asked, disappointed.

"Give me some credit, Meera! I kept knocking."

"Go on…"

"The door opened and a man yelled at me. He wasn't even dressed. He was wearing a torn undershirt and boxers. There was a beer can in his hand and he must have had a few already."

"What did he say?"

"He yelled at me again."

"I suppose you had to leave then?"

"No. I saw a gun tucked into his waistband. Then I fled."

"What? Oh my God, Becky! Are you alright?"

I felt guilty, putting Becky in harm's way.

"I was a bit shaken up at first," Becky laughed nervously. "I think my car drove itself out of there. But I'm okay now."

"So you never got to meet Anna then."

"When did I say that, Meera? You're rushing ahead."

I dialed it back a bit.

"So what happened after you got back to the diner?"

"About two hours later, this Anna Collins came to the diner."

"Does she come there often? I don't remember seeing her."

"Nope. But Sylvie knew who she was of course."

"Did she just come in to eat?"

"No! She asked to see me. Or rather, the young chit who had come knocking on her door. She didn't know it was me exactly."

"So that guy must have told her someone came knocking."

"Told her? Complained to her, most likely."

"So you finally got to talk to her."

There was a pause. I imagined Becky nodding her head.

"She told me a thing or two, more like."

"And what's that?"

"She said she saw Leo jump out of the window and get away in Charlie's car. She was sure it was Leo and no one was going to convince her otherwise."

"Did she say what time it was?"

"7:30 PM."

"Exactly 7:30? Not 7:29 or 7:31? How can she be sure of that?"

"That's what she said."

"And she came to the diner to tell you this? Why?"

"We talked about that, Sylvie and I. It seems a bit strange, doesn't it?"

"What else did this Anna say?"

"She reminded us she had already talked to the police. And they had arrested Leo based on it. So the case was closed. Leo killed Charlie."

"She can keep saying that all she wants. That doesn't make it true."

"Exactly!" Becky burst out. "Sylvie says her son's a crook."

"Yeah! Stan said something about it. You better stay away from that guy, Becky."

I couldn't bear it if something happened to Becky.

"Did you get to ask Anna any questions?"

"She wouldn't listen. All she would say when I mentioned Charlie was that he was dead and he couldn't harm anyone now."

"What's that supposed to mean?"

Becky's voice grew thoughtful.

"She seemed relieved Charlie wasn't around anymore."

"That means she didn't get along with Charlie."

Becky agreed with me. It seemed Sylvie thought that too. I had always had doubts about what Anna Collins had seen that night. I figured she couldn't be sure if the person jumping out of the window was Leo. Maybe there hadn't been any such person at all.

"Anna Collins could be lying about the whole thing."

"How are you going to prove that, Meera?"

"We either have to make her talk, or find someone else who will contradict her."

"I'm not any help at all, am I?" Becky said glumly.

"What? You are my eyes and ears in Swan Creek, Becks. You're doing great."

"Audrey didn't turn up today," Becky said next.

"Don't worry. Maybe she'll be in tomorrow."

I wished Becky goodnight and hung up. The phone rang before I had a moment to reflect over what she had said. It was Stan.

Chapter 12

"Leo may be getting out on bail," Stan began.

I was flabbergasted. All this time, we had assumed Leo was on his own. Who was posting bail for him?

"But how?"

"By the usual process, Meera!"

"I mean, who's paying up for him?"

"Some lawyer," Stan said. "But I don't know who he's working for."

"Did you ask Leo?"

"He's as surprised as we are."

"Maybe I can at least talk to him then."

Leo had been the closest to Charlie. He was best equipped to tell us anything about Charlie's lifestyle and his habits.

"Can you get him to confess?"

"I just want to find out what really happened. I still think Leo's innocent. But if he's responsible, I won't let him get away."

It had taken me some time to come to terms with this concept. But I had to think like that if I wanted to be objective.

"Did you find out anything new?" Stan asked.

He seemed eager for information.

"Not a lot. Can't do much from a thousand miles away."

"Any little bit will be more than what we have right now, Meera."

"Well, Charlie was a cold fish. He didn't spread any cheer around, that's for sure. He wasn't rude, but neither was he warm and fuzzy."

"That sounds like the man I knew."

"Audrey Jones is lazy and incompetent. She had an exclusive contract to work for Charlie Gibson only, but she did other work on the sly."

"You're talking about that housekeeper of his?"

"Yes, Stan. A housekeeper who is suddenly flush with money."

"How do you know that?"

"She's acting like a lady of leisure, turning up for coffee at the diner. She's never been able to afford that before, apparently."

"She's got a lot of time on her hands now," Stan mused.

"Don't you see, Stan? You think someone stole money from Charlie. Leo says he didn't. Now here's a person who has more money than she should. Maybe it was Audrey who dipped into Charlie's wallet?"

"You're saying she killed him for the money?"

"Not exactly! But she could have taken the money before she called the cops."

"I suppose that's possible," Stan relented. "I'll talk to her."

"Anna Collins is a bit too eager to pin the crime on Leo."

"How so?"

"Well, I sent Becky to go look around Charlie's house."

"What's there to look for, Meera?"

"We'll find out soon, won't we? So anyway, Becky knocked on Anna's door. She wasn't in but she turned up at the diner later, just to tell Becky she saw Leo jump out of the window."

"Hmm…" Stan was noncommittal.

"What kind of outdoor lights does Charlie Gibson have?"

"Where are you going with this?"

"Anna says she saw Leo at 7:30 PM. It's barely Spring and it's dark at 7:30. How could she be sure it was Leo? Does Charlie have a brightly lit yard, or one of those motion detectors?"

Stan let out an expletive.

"We never checked on that."

Stan Miller misses a lot of things. But he's at least becoming amenable to suggestions. The Stan Miller I knew a year ago wouldn't even have entertained this idea.

"How many other neighbors does Charlie have?"

"The usual, I suppose."

What I meant to ask was how many of them had the police talked to. I had to spell it out for Stan.

"Well, we were going to interview the people who have houses in the cul de sac. Then Anna Collins came forward."

"And you took her at her word."

Stan was quiet.

"She seems to be happy Charlie's gone. What did she have against him? Did they have some kind of feud going on?"

Stan obviously didn't know the answer to that.

"I'm going to talk to her tomorrow," he said with some resolve.

"Let's say Leo did not take the money. Actually, leave the money out of this completely. What did anyone gain by killing Charlie Gibson?"

"What's the motive, you mean?" Stan asked.

I let him stew over it for a while.

"Did Charlie do anything out of the ordinary the last few days of his life? What was his routine? Who did he talk to other than Leo or Audrey?"

"I'm going to talk to those neighbors tomorrow," Stan promised.

I hung up and sat back on my bed, leaning against the counterpane. There had to be more information out there about Charlie. What was I missing? I remembered my craft store purchase and took it out.

"What's that?" Jeet asked.

I took out a stack of index cards and some colored pens. These would have to do in the absence of a white board. I made a card for Charlie Gibson, Leo Smith, Anna Collins and Audrey Jones. These were the only people we had come across so far.

I picked up Charlie's card first and wrote out what I had learned about him. I wrote his schedule on the back of the card.

"Pappa thinks Charlie didn't talk much. But there have to be things he knows. They have known each other all these years."

Tony looked at me.

"Want to go and talk to him?"

"Why not?"

Pappa would probably shoo me out this late at night but it was a chance worth taking. I knocked on Motee Ba's door and went in. Pappa was sitting up in bed, snug under the covers. Some old Hollywood movie was playing on the TV. He was sipping brandy and hot water from a glass. It is the Patel family remedy for a cold, actual or imagined.

"Your Pappa's sniffling a bit."

Motee Ba confirmed my suspicions.

"Can we talk for a while?" I asked Pappa.

He made a face but he didn't say no. I plunged ahead.

"I'm trying to piece together what Charlie did on his last day. And also what he may have done the last few days before he died."

"Go on," Pappa said.

"Sylvie said he went to the library before he had lunch. And he did that every Tuesday."

"He had things marked for every day of the week. He did one or two chores every day. Kept him busy, he said."

"What did he do the rest of the day?"

"Went for a walk, watched TV, walked that dog of his."

I had completely forgotten about the dog.

"He has a dog, right? I guess he had to walk him at least twice a day."

"What are you getting at, girl?"

I wasn't quite sure.

"Did he ever mention someone called Anna?"

Pappa didn't remember much. Then he sat up straight.

"Bank day!" he exclaimed. "Wednesday was bank day. He went to the bank and withdrew a hundred dollars for weekly expenses."

"What would they be?"

"How do I know?" Pappa boomed. "Groceries, gas, miscellaneous stuff…"

"He must be spending almost all of it by Tuesday evening."

"He barely had ten dollars left," Pappa nodded. "And whatever he had, he put in a box for savings."

"Any idea what he did with it?"

Pappa shrugged, looking impatient.

I bid them goodnight and we went back to our room.

"I've never agreed with this idea that Leo stole money," I mused. "Stan said they recognized one of the bills Leo had, remember?"

"You think this was left over from the 100 Charlie got from the bank?" Tony asked.

Was that the only money Leo had? Stan hadn't mentioned that. I called him again.

"Leo had 70 odd dollars with him," Stan said in a sleepy voice. "And he says he spent around 20-30 on gas and food on the road."

"There's no way it could all have come out of Charlie's weekly expenses."

I told Stan about the $100 Charlie withdrew from the bank each Wednesday.

"This is a puzzle alright. Of course, Leo still maintains Charlie gave him the money."

"Can you find out how much Charlie withdrew from the bank last week?"

Stan promised to add that to his list of things to do. It was growing by the minute.

Jeet was fast asleep when I hung up the phone. Tony was lying flat on his bed, looking drowsy.

"How come Leo never asked you for a job?"

Kids from town often turn up at Tony's gas station, looking to make an extra buck.

Tony turned on his side and yawned.

"Did you hear Leo's getting out on bail?"

Tony sat up after that.

"So someone's taking care of him after all."

"But who is it and where were they all this time?"

Tony didn't have an answer for that.

"I can't wait to talk to Leo," I groaned.

"You can do that tomorrow morning," Tony said pointedly.

I shuffled the cards in my hands. I remembered the twitching curtain Becky had mentioned. There was one more person we could talk to. I placed a question mark on one card. Becky would have to go talk to this person.

I changed into my jammies and tried to settle down. My mind buzzed with questions. I wished I could drink some herbal tea to calm down. The little electric clock on the nightstand read 12:30. We were meeting for breakfast in the hotel dining room at 7 AM. My back ached from the hours spent in the car. I really needed to sleep.

My eyes fell on the packet of photos. I began looking through them again. An earlier memory resurfaced. I peered closely at a photo. There it was, the small symbol I had noticed in the restroom. But the photo was from the campground in the mountains of New Mexico. I found another small doodle in a different photo. We were standing close to a sign that said Welcome to New Mexico. And there it was, a small circle with long and short lines radiating from it. It looked like the sun to me.

I skipped through the photos rapidly and arranged them in an order, starting from the few we had taken in Oklahoma. I looked at each of them closely. Some of them had these small doodles in the queerest places, on sidewalks, walls of gas stations, or picnic tables at the visitor's center. I had come across some 5-6 different symbols. I didn't know what else to call them. I could make no sense out of them.

Finally, my mind couldn't handle the overload. My eyelids grew heavy and I settled into a dreamless sleep as the hour struck 2 AM.

Chapter 13

Tremors rippled through my bed and a cacophony of crashing cymbals forced me awake. I buried my head in my pillow, trying to get away from this inhuman onslaught on my senses. The noise went up and I couldn't take it anymore.

I peeped through an eye at a crazy sight. The TV was cranked up high with some heavy metal song. Tony and Jeet, freshly showered, were singing along, jumping around the room, miming along with the video. Jeet saw me and gave a Tarzan like yell.

"You're in so much trouble, Meera," he crowed, pointing to the clock by my bedside.

The red LED lights couldn't be right, could they? It was 6:45 and I had barely slept a wink. I looked around and found the printed photos, arranged in neat piles. I had dreamt of being on some kind of treasure hunt, trying to decode symbols on pillars and walls. I remembered arranging the photos in a certain order. So it wasn't just my imagination. I couldn't separate dreams from reality at that point.

I shooed the boys out and rushed into the shower. Of course they had run through all the hot water. I shivered under the freezing jets but they helped clear the cobwebs from my head. I pulled on a clean pair of jeans and dressed in layers. The day would get warmer before it turned cold again.

The phone rang as I was swiping my lips with some gloss. It was Becky. Luckily for me, she got to the point.

"Audrey was here."

I looked at the clock and realized Becky was an hour ahead.

"She ordered the breakfast special," Becky whispered.

I had no interest in what Audrey Jones put in her body. I am not her doctor or fitness trainer.

"Did you talk to her?" I asked, trying not to sound impatient.

"I told her we knew she was working for other people. She denied it at first. Then she said she wasn't going to upset people by turning them down."

"What about that contract with Charlie?"

"She agreed to that 20 years ago when Charlie first hired her. She figured he must have forgotten about it by now."

"But why did she take on the other jobs? Did she need the money?"

"Not really, she said. Charlie paid her very well. She got bored."

I tried to make sense of that. Becky explained.

"Charlie didn't let her watch TV. He didn't chat with her. She liked getting away for a change of scene."

"More like a chance to gossip," I muttered. "Did you ask her about Charlie's schedule?"

"You could set your clock by him," Becky went on. "He made his own breakfast every day. Then he took that dog of his for a walk. He walked for an hour or so. Then he did his chore of the day."

"Pappa told me about that. He had a task specified for every day, it seems."

"Tuesday was for the library," Becky droned on. "Groceries twice a week. And there was other stuff I don't remember."

"When did Audrey go to work?"

"He let her in before he went for this morning walk. She was to have his snack ready by 10:15. Then he went out again at 11."

"So she went in and made a snack for him first."

"No, she made lunch. The snack was juice and a muffin that was store bought. Sometimes he came in to Sylvie's for coffee."

I tried to imagine such a cut and dried schedule. I am not built that way. Every day has to offer something new.

"So what? She cleaned the house and made lunch?"

"That's right. Charlie ate lunch at home except on Tuesdays and Wednesdays. Then he napped. Audrey was supposed to make herself scarce at this time."

"You mean she had to go out of the house?"

"I'm not sure about that," Becky said. "But I think so. She wasn't allowed to put her feet up or guess what, watch TV. Other people let her do that, it seems."

I remembered what Aunt Reema had said. Other people probably weren't around to keep an eye on her. So she did as she pleased. It looked like Audrey's other jobs were just a place to while away time.

"Then what? She went back?"

"Right. She got dinner while Charlie walked that dog again. Dinner was at 6:30. She just served it at once on the table and left."

"Did she talk about Leo at all?"

"He helped her with some of her chores when Charlie wasn't around."

Audrey had provided a fair idea of what a day in Charlie Gibson's life looked like. Was any of it going to help me get to the truth?

"What else, Becky?"

"I may have mentioned Anna Collins," Becky said.

I could sense she was holding back on the real thing.

"Spit it out, sister!"

"You won't believe this, Meera. You know Anna's son, that scary guy? We knew he's a bad one. But we didn't know how bad. He's been to jail thrice."

"Did she say why?"

"Domestic violence, theft, creating disturbances, all kinds of nasty stuff."

"Audrey told you that?"

"Charlie couldn't stand the sight of him. He called the cops on that Don guy more than once. He even gave evidence against him."

"I'm sure Anna wasn't pleased with that?"

"You bet. Audrey said they had a big fight. Don threatened to get even but the cops took him away. Anna vowed she would avenge her son some day."

"Do you believe her? I mean, Audrey? Maybe she was fibbing."

"Oh no! A couple of old timers were having coffee at the next table. They were nodding along, saying they remembered."

"So they were Charlie's neighbors?"

"I don't think so. This happened at the supermarket."

So Anna had threatened Charlie in front of plenty of people. Chances were, she was just letting off steam. I didn't have a mental image of Anna.

"Do you think this Anna Collins is capable of harming anyone?"

"No way!" Becky pressed. "She stares at her feet and mumbles. I don't see her stabbing anyone, even in a fit of anger."

"What about Don? Don's out of jail, isn't he?"

"Now him…he actually looks like a killer."

"Wow! I have to tell Stan about this."

"You do that, Meera."

I remembered the twitching curtains. I talked to Becky about them.

"I'll try to swing by later today," she promised.

I promised to take plenty of pictures at the Grand Canyon. Then I told her about Leo.

"Leo's getting out?" she sounded shocked. "Sylvie will be glad to know that. Talk to her."

Sylvie came on the line and enquired about everyone. She got worked up when I told her Leo was getting out of jail.

"They should never have taken him in. But you know how our police are. And you aren't here this time to keep them straight."

I assured her I was trying to get to the bottom of things.

"Sylvie, do you think you can invite Leo over for a meal at the diner? Give him some chores?"

"Keep him busy, you mean?" Sylvie asked, catching on. "Don't you worry, baby girl. I'll take him over to our place. He's got no business going back to that nasty house anyway."

I thanked Sylvie profusely. Jon and Sylvie are simple folk but they are the kindest people I know. Sylvie would see that Leo was fed and had a roof over his head.

There was a loud rap on the door and I hung up, wishing Sylvie a nice day.

"You're late, Meera!" Dad frowned, showing me his watch.

I followed him to the hotel's café. It was 7:30 AM and it looked like everyone was already done with breakfast. They were on their second cup of coffee.

"What were you doing all this time?" Dad asked, refusing to let go.

"I overslept," I muttered, slathering cream cheese on my bagel.

I slid a couple of fried eggs and a sausage patty on a bagel half and doused it in red hot sauce. I slapped the other half of the bagel on top, making my own egg and bagel sandwich. I took a huge bite and washed it down with lukewarm coffee.

"You know this is the first vacation we have taken in years."

Dad was in a mood alright.

"It's really important for our family. I don't want you messing it up with any of your shenanigans."

I bristled under this unexpected attack. It didn't seem fair to me.

"What am I doing, Dad? Really? Do you see me lying drunk somewhere or beating people up?"

Dad's face turned red. He wasn't used to his kids talking back to him.

Motee Ba placed a gentle hand on my arm. Sally's eyes had clouded, sensing trouble. Jeet's eyes were bright, and he was sitting up, ready to snitch on me if needed.

"No need to be dramatic," Dad said dryly. "You know very well what I'm talking about."

"She's on the phone all night long," Jeet sang out.

He always lives up to my expectations.

Dad pursed his lips and pinched his forehead.

"I'm warning you, Meera. You are getting out of hand."

This is the time when Pappa usually joins forces with Dad. He taps his cane and promises all kinds of consequences if I don't fall in line. He was quiet this time.

Of course Dad noticed that. He turned to Pappa next.

"You have to stop encouraging her, Pappa."

I was getting a splitting headache. I stood up, grabbed my bagel sandwich in one hand, picked up a pot of yogurt in the other, and walked away. There's only so much I can take on an empty stomach.

I heard Motee Ba and Dad begin to murmur behind my back. My grandma would try to smooth things out. Sally hadn't said a word all this time. If she was wise, she wouldn't take sides.

I devoted myself to my breakfast, meager as it was. I went over everything Becky had told me. What was Audrey doing spending ten bucks on breakfast at the diner? Could she really have taken money from Charlie's wallet?

The phone rang as I chewed over the last bite of my sandwich. I didn't recognize the number but the area code was Swan Creek. Leo's voice came over the line and I heaved a sigh of relief.

Chapter 14

"How are you, Leo?" I burst out. "It's good to hear your voice."

Leo thanked me for my concern.

"They just let me go. That policeman gave me your number. I hope it's okay to call."

I assured him it was fine.

"Do you know who got you out on bail?"

"Not yet. But I'm assuming whoever it is will get in touch."

"Maybe it's one of your friends?"

Leo laughed nervously.

"My friends don't have this kind of money, Meera. And I don't have any relatives. I'm all alone in this world."

I didn't know what to say to that.

"Sylvie's waiting for you," I began. "She and Jon will take care of you for a while. You don't have to go back to that place."

"That place is the only home I have known in a long time, Meera."

I wondered if I had offended him in some way.

"Right. I just thought you might not want to go there. You know, since…"

Since it was the scene of a murder? What do you say at such times?

"You are very kind, Meera."

I sensed he was getting emotional.

"Look, Leo. You don't have to worry about a thing. March is almost over, right. Sylvie and Jon will put you up through the summer. And then you can come stay with us until you go off to college or get a job. Or whatever it is you want to do."

"I don't know what to say."

"No need to say anything. Just get your stuff and head to Sylvie's."

"You don't know anything about me," Leo hesitated.

"We know you're a good kid. That's enough for us."

"Thanks Meera!"

Leo was quiet for a moment. Then he asked the burning question.

"Do you have any leads?"

"I wish I was there in Swan Creek," I admitted. "It's kind of hard, trying to find out stuff from a distance. But I am trying to manage it."

"How can I help you?"

"I have loads of questions for you," I gushed. "Now that you're free, free to talk, I mean, we can go over them."

"Just fire away, Meera!"

I grabbed the bull by the horns.

"How did you get all that money? Stan said Charlie gave it to you?"

"That's right. I found out my friends were in the area just before dinner time. I hadn't met them in quite some time. Charlie told me to take the car and go. He gave me some money for the road."

"How much?"

"Just over a 100 bucks," Leo said.

He seemed to smile at the memory.

"I don't have an official Spring Break since I am homeschooled. Charlie wanted me to go have some fun."

I cleared my throat.

"Leo, don't take this the wrong way. Pappa said Charlie went to the bank once a week on Wednesdays. And he withdrew $100 for weekly expenses. Did he go to the bank or ATM twice that week?"

Leo laughed.

"He handed over his piggy bank. Asked me to take whatever was in it. It was like a lottery, he said."

"And you got over a hundred bucks out of it?"

"Yeah! Isn't that cool? Charlie put whatever was left out of his weekly budget into that box. A few dollars at a time."

"Did he give you any more money?"

"He gave me an extra twenty bucks to get some munchies for the road."

"Why didn't you explain all this to the cops?"

"They asked me if I took money from Charlie's wallet. I didn't. But they don't believe me."

"Was anyone around when Charlie gave you that money?"

"Audrey. She was setting the table for dinner."

"What time did you leave?"

"A little after 7 PM. Dinner was light on Tuesdays because Charlie had meatloaf for lunch. Audrey made some sandwiches and heated up soup."

"When did she leave?"

"She left at 6:30 just as we sat down for dinner."

"Did Charlie seem excited? Different in any way?"

"He smiled a couple of times."

"Was that odd?"

"Kind of. Charlie wasn't very expressive, you know."

"Did you ask him what he was smiling about?"

Leo sounded apologetic.

"I wasn't paying attention. I just wanted to finish dinner and hit the road."

"How long were you planning to be away?"

"I didn't really have any concrete plans at the time. Charlie insisted I spend the night instead of driving back. He said I didn't have to hurry back."

"What did he usually do after dinner?"

"He watched TV. He let Bandit out once around 8 PM. Then he went to his room and read until 10."

I had some more information about Charlie's routine.

There was a rap on the door and Tony burst in. He grinned when he saw me on the phone.

"Time to go," he mouthed.

I wracked my brain for any other quick questions for Leo.

"Does Charlie have any family?"

"He never mentioned anyone," Leo said.

I thought about Charlie's will.

"Wasn't he thinking about leaving everything to you?"

Leo didn't know anything about that. I reminded him to get in touch with Sylvie. He promised to go over as soon as he showered and got his stuff together.

"Take care, Leo," I said, feeling a sudden pang of emotion.

"We need to leave," Tony warned. "Uncle Andy's not happy with you."

"I sort of guessed that, Tony."

In for a penny, in for a pound, I decided. I dialed Stan's phone and hoped he would answer.

"I'm in a bit of a hurry," I started.

I told him how Charlie had given Leo the money. Then I told him about Anna threatening Charlie Gibson in front of a crowd.

"How do you find out such stuff, Meera?" Stan said in wonder.

"So Anna Collins had some kind of grudge against Charlie. Maybe she's lying to hide something?"

"You think she killed Charlie?"

"I don't know, Stan. I wish I had met that woman. But Becky says she's meek as a mouse."

"She appears to be," Stan mused.

"Her son looks more likely. He's been to jail many times and Charlie put him there."

Stan promised to check up on Don Collins. I hung up and literally ran to the car. Everyone was in their seats, and Tony was behind the wheel. I climbed up in the passenger seat and stared ahead, refusing to make eye contact with Dad.

"We're going to miss the show," Jeet complained. "All because of you, Meera."

"What show?"

"The IMAX movie!"

"We're watching a movie?" I tried to sound really bored. I had never been to an IMAX theatre and the whole experience sounded exciting.

"They have one every hour, don't they?" Tony asked, trying to diffuse the tension.

I blinked at him, mouthing a silent thank you.

"Waiting an extra hour upsets our schedule," Dad said, sounding just like Jeet. "We have to do the entire Desert View Trail, allowing time for snacks and lunch and reach Hopi Point before sunset."

I sneaked a look in the rearview mirror. Dad was really worked up. Sally put a hand on his knee and smiled at him. His anger seemed to evaporate. He put his hand over hers and cooed something softly. I couldn't hear what he was saying, and I didn't want to.

Tony merged onto Highway 64, the road leading us to the Grand Canyon. A line of cars stretched ahead of us and I realized they were all going to the same place. Maybe we could beat the crowds if we were late everywhere. Then I saw the bunch of cars behind us and knew that wasn't happening.

"The weather's cooperating," Tony noted. "It hasn't snowed in a week and there's a high of 60F today. We should be able to get to all the points on the drive."

Spring Break is a bit early to visit the canyon. But you get to beat the really big crowds. We had talked about this. No one wanted to miss going to the Grand Canyon. I allowed myself to relax as I realized where I was. Motee Ba seemed to read my mind.

"We're finally here. Can you believe it?"

I thought of Leo and how uncertain his future was. The Patels were doing very well compared to that. So our tempers ran high once in a while. So what?

The car sped through the miles on the long straight road, rising and dipping periodically. Tony pulled into the theater parking lot an hour later. Dad and Jeet rushed ahead to get the tickets. I helped Pappa down and leaned forward to whisper in his ear.

"Leo's out on bail."

His face lit up in a smile.

"I talked to Sylvie. They are ready to welcome him. Leo's going to get his stuff and head over there now."

"That's a relief," Motee Ba said. "Have you made any progress?"

There wasn't much time to give them a full report.

"Stan's checking up on a few things for me. We'll get there, Motee Ba."

"Your Dad will be fine, Meera. Don't worry."

She couldn't bear the thought of father and daughter arguing over anything. In her own way, she was telling me to take it easy.

Sally gave me one of her smiles. I ignored her.

Tony shook his head, letting me know I wasn't being cool.

"You can sulk all day or you can have a good time."

I wanted to have a good time. But I was hungry. And hunger is something I haven't been able to ignore yet. Tony walked ahead and stood in a line. He came back with a steaming hot cinnamon roll loaded with icing. I tore off one buttery layer and breathed in the heady aroma. The sugar dissolved on my tongue and I felt my tension recede.

"You know me so well."

I waited a second until Tony's arm came around me and I snuggled into him. Sally gave me a smile, a different one. This time I smiled back.

We were just in time for the 9:30 show.

Chapter 15

The IMAX movie was mind blowing. It stayed with me long after we got into the car and lined up near the park entrance. Our car finally came up to the ranger's cabin and we got our entry pass. Tony headed to the visitor center, and we collected some brochures and looked around.

I warmed my hands with a cup of coffee.

"We need to talk," I said to Tony.

"Anything urgent?" he asked. "Why don't you try to live in the moment, Meera? At least for today?"

I wanted to tell Tony about the little doodles I had noticed. Had he seen them too? Maybe he didn't notice them but he would remember if I showed him the photos. Then I realized the photos were back in the hotel room.

"Okay. There's a lot to tell you but it can wait. There's just one thing I want to talk about right now."

Dad walked up to us just then, sipping his coffee, and I clammed up. Tony was already widening his eyes, warning me to stay quiet.

"That was some movie, wasn't it?" Dad asked.

It was his way of trying to mend fences with me. He turned toward Tony.

"You guys have plenty of room on the camera? And extra film and batteries?"

Tony nodded.

"Why don't you handle this?" Dad handed over a camcorder to Tony.

I didn't know where it came from.

"I want to capture this trip in every way possible," Dad said shyly. "Your mother and I bought the video camera last night.

It's charged and ready to go."

"You went out after dinner?"

"We were talking until late. That's when we realized we should have one of these. Luckily, there was a 24 hour store nearby."

"That's cool, Uncle Andy!" Tony cried. "You know what, I was wishing we had one of these when we rode the cable car up that mountain. And when Meera ate a bunch of those chilies and couldn't stop fanning her mouth for hours."

Dad and Tony high fived each other.

"Let's get going," Pappa said, tapping his cane.

The first point was right near the Visitor Center. We couldn't walk fast enough to get our first glimpse. Motee Ba clutched my arm and stared at the majestic rock formation ahead of us. Her eyes were moist with unshed tears. Dad stood a few feet away, his arm around Sally.

Photos were called for and we posed and pouted in different spots. Tony was busy recording a video of the area.

We decided to stop for a snack somewhere on the way. There was a deli at the end of the trail and we would eat there later. Tony parked near a picnic area and Sally and Motee Ba pulled some bags out. There was some fresh fruit left over from the farmer's market. Sally poured water in paper cups, insisting we drink it.

Pappa chewed noisily on something my aunt had sent.

"Eat up, kids," he ordered. "This is real Gujarati food. Not like that orange dust."

"Hasn't that gone bad yet?" I wrinkled my nose. "How long ago did Aunt Anita send it?"

"*Dhebras* stay good for over 10 days," Pappa said defensively, holding up the fried bread he was eating. "Tell her, Hansa!"

He stared at my grandma, waiting for her to explain.

"Your Pappa's right, Meera. These are made to last long."

"Tell her!" Pappa boomed. "We snacked on these on our 10 day voyage, every time we traveled home to India."

Motee Ba has often told us about these epic sea voyages. Traveling by train from inland Africa to the Mombasa port, then boarding a steam ship that would take nine days and nine nights to reach Bombay. She carried huge boxes of *chevdo*, *laddus* and *dhebras* as snacks to last them all this time. They got 3 meals a day on the ship too, so they must have had a really good appetite.

I bit into the fried bread-like thing to pacify Pappa. Made with millet flour, it's a bit chewy. The garlic hit me first, followed by crunchy sesame seeds and sour tamarind. I piled two plates high with food and took one plate to Tony.

We walked over to the edge and sat down, enjoying the scene before us.

Tony bit into a juicy peach and looked around. He leaned toward me and whispered.

"Okay, Meera, what were you saying? Tell me one thing, just one."

I chose to talk about the symbols.

"Have you noticed any drawings or doodles anywhere?"

"You mean like graffiti?" he asked.

"Much smaller," I explained. "And isolated."

I told him how I had noticed one on a restroom mirror and then another one on pillars outside the rest area.

"Is it like some folk art? Something to do with Arizona?"

I banged my fist on the bench, excited.

"That's what I thought too. But get this! I was looking at all our photos last night, and I noticed a couple in New Mexico too. And in Texas."

"Maybe it's a road trip thing?" Tony mused. "You know how kids get bored cooped up in the car? And they like to draw all the time. I guess they just act out when they stop somewhere."

"Why didn't I think of that?"

Tony laughed and punched me lightly in the arm.

"You tend to ignore the simple solutions, Meera. Everything is a big conspiracy."

I thought for a moment. Maybe Tony was right. I didn't appreciate his comment though. What he meant was I blew things out of proportion. That is so not true.

"Leo just…"

Tony balanced his plate on his knees and covered his ears with his hands.

"Just one thing, Meera. You had your chance."

"Who's being dramatic now?" I huffed.

We collected all the trash in a bag and stowed it in the car. I decided to drive. The next point on the trail was some five miles away. The road wound in serpentine fashion. All we saw were plenty of trees and shrubs on both sides of the road. The road was single lane with a lower speed limit so I got plenty of opportunity to chat with everyone.

They were talking about how Jeet was having a great Spring Break before heading off to college. The apple doesn't fall far from the tree, they say. Jeet has been accepted by a bunch of Ivy League schools and is heading to Harvard in the fall. He's enjoying being pampered by everyone before he leaves home.

I spotted the sign for Grandview Point which was our next stop. This spot offered a panoramic view of the canyon from east to west. Jeet lived up to his snarky self.

"It's the same pile of rocks we saw earlier."

"This is millions of years of evolution, son," Dad said, sounding disappointed.

He's always ready to get into a pedantic mode.

"You see those different layers? The green, the brown, the red? They are all different types of rocks. Most of it is sedimentary rock from the Paleozoic period."

"Okay Dad!" Jeet said.

He had spotted an outcropping of rock he wanted to climb. He went off with Tony, ordering me to take plenty of pictures when they scaled it.

The next stop was another five miles away. This one had awesome views of the Colorado river. I realized I was witnessing something that was so much bigger than myself. I breathed in the cool, fresh air and took a good look around. Motee Ba and Pappa were standing arm in arm, pointing things out to each other. Dad stood a few feet next to Sally, staring at the view in between stealing glances at her. Sally had her usual angelic smile on her face.

I heard a yell and turned to see Jeet and Tony waving at me from a distance. I began taking pictures, purging my mind of any thoughts of Swan Creek.

We finally reached the Desert View Watch Tower which is the last point on the trail. Tony, Jeet and I rushed to the top to take more photos. The view from the top was mesmerizing.

"How was it?" Motee Ba asked when we finally went down to the car.

"Outstanding," Jeet told her. "Don't worry. We shot a video and Meera clicked plenty of pictures."

I turned to take a last look at the tower and stumbled. Tony caught my arm. I grabbed his hand and pulled him along as I walked back to the tower.

"Where are you going now, Meera?" Dad asked with irritation. "It's time to go."

I ignored him and rushed to a point at the base of a tower.

"See that?" I asked Tony. "That's what I'm talking about."

"I don't see anything," Tony said, looking around.

I pointed to a small flower with a curve drawn below it, sort of like a smiley. It looked like the flower was smiling.

Tony shook his head.

"That's just a silly doodle. Come on! Didn't you see all those drawings on the walls inside?"

"They are historic drawings – art. This is not art."

"Exactly!" Tony put his hands on his hips. "It's vandalism, Meera."

"You still don't think this is important?"

"Maybe it is some kind of secret code," Tony said. "So what? What's it got do with you? With us?"

Dad called out to us again. His pitch was higher this time.

"Uncle Andy is trying to be patient," Tony warned.

I followed Tony back to the car and got in.

"Why are you sulking now, girl?" Pappa asked as I slid in next to him.

"We have an hour's drive to the sunset point," Dad said, reading from a map. "We have to get there by 4:30 if we want to get a good spot."

It was a little over 3 PM.

"What about lunch?" Pappa complained.

"I have an idea," Motee Ba said eagerly.

She whispered something to Sally. Sally smiled back, nodding her head.

"Take us to a picnic area," Motee Ba ordered Dad.

We parked near a different area this time. Luckily we could snag an empty table. Many like minded people were hogging all the picnic areas along the road.

We scampered down and Motee Ba directed the boys to unload a bunch of bags from the car. She handed me a knife and chopping board and a bunch of onions. Don't ask me where she got the onions from!

One of the coveted qualities of an Indian bride is the ability to chop onions really fine. So of course Motee Ba has trained me in this. I had a pile of chopped onions ready within minutes. A few tomatoes were added and I made quick work of cutting them down too.

Tony was emptying a two pound bag of puffed rice into a big plastic bin.

"Are we making Bhel Poori?" I cried.

Motee Ba smiled, clearing up the mystery. A cheer went up. Bhel Poori is one of our favorite snacks. It's hot, sweet, tangy and just yum. Tony and Jeet began dumping some fried noodles and snack mixes into the container. In went the onions and tomatoes. Sally handed me cans of boiled potatoes. I chopped them and they went in too. Then Sally handed me fresh green Hatch chilies and I diced them fine before adding them in.

Motee Ba began mixing everything up with her hands. She actually forgot to bring spatulas!

Finally the coup de grace was delivered. I opened a big bottle of date and tamarind chutney and poured it over the mix in the canister. Everything came together to form Bhel, one of the most popular street foods of India.

"I didn't know we had all these fixings with us," I said, chomping down a big handful to taste the seasonings.

We ladled this out in big paper bowls and everyone sat back to enjoy the Bhel.

"You know, I took your mother to Chowpatty when we first met," Dad said, sounding sentimental.

Chowpatty is an iconic beach in the city of Mumbai, formerly Bombay.

"We shared a cup of Bhel and I told her about life in America."

He looked at Sally. For once, Sally wasn't smiling. She had a speculative look on her face.

"How do you like your Bhel?" Dad asked Sally.

"It tastes familiar," she said.

My Motee Ba said a small prayer under her breath and smiled at Sally. Maybe this trip to the Grand Canyon would be memorable for more than one reason.

Chapter 16

Everyone seemed to be in a good mood after the meal. We shuffled back into the car, wasting a few minutes over who wanted to sit where.

Dad kept glancing at his watch.

"We're going to be late."

"Relax Dad, it's just 30 or so miles to that sunset point," Jeet said, reading from a brochure.

"Wait for a few minutes, Jeet," Dad said grimly. "You'll see what I mean."

Dad took the wheel and we merged onto the road. A mile down the road, another car got in ahead of us. Cars joined the main trail road from the numerous scenic points and picnic areas that dotted the road. They were all lining up to watch the sunset, of course.

"Is there only one place to watch the sunset from?" I asked.

"There are a couple of places," Dad said. "But you see how many people are here?"

My phone emitted some kind of beep and grew silent. I had begun to think of it as my phone now, although it was currently resting in Tony's pocket. I looked at him hopefully and he shook his head. I guessed he wasn't going to risk annoying Dad.

"What's that noise?" Pappa asked.

No one said anything.

Five minutes later, we had barely covered a quarter mile. Cars stretched ahead of us bumper to bumper now.

"It's 4 PM," Motee Ba said.

"I know, Ba!" Dad said, frustrated.

He turned around and frowned at Pappa.

"You just had to stop and eat, didn't you? We could have eaten after we reached Hopi Point."

Pappa put a lid on his mouth for a change and didn't say a word.

We covered another mile and came across more cars trying to merge in from one of the scenic overlooks. A light drizzle started and a groan went up.

"That does it!" Jeet chortled.

The phone dinged again and I forced myself to ignore it.

"We'll have to spend one more day here if we can't see the sunset today," Dad began. "You can't come to the Grand Canyon and not watch the sunset. We may never come here again!"

Tony and Jeet exchanged looks. They were getting impatient to get to the next point of the trip.

"Sounds boring," Jeet began. "We've already seen all the rocks we can today."

"We can take in a trail tomorrow," Dad said eagerly. "Nothing too strenuous. Just a 2-3 mile one. The view changes as you head down into the canyon, Jeet. There are vistas below that can't be seen from the top. Don't you remember the movie?"

"Exactly! We already saw the interior of the canyon in the movie."

The drizzle eased up and a watery sun peeped out. Maybe it would have mercy on us after all.

There was another ding and Dad banged his hand on the steering wheel.

"What is that sound?"

"I think it's my phone," Tony admitted.

"There must be a missed call," I added boldly. "The phone will keep beeping until I check it."

Dad waved a hand in the air, giving me permission. But I noticed his ears were turning red. I grabbed the phone as soon as Tony pulled it out of his pocket and flipped it open. It wasn't from a saved contact but the area code was Swan Creek. Then I recognized the number from that morning.

"It's Leo," I said, just loudly enough for Tony to hear it.

"Why is that boy calling you?" Dad demanded.

"I don't know, Dad!"

"Didn't I ask you to stay away from anything related to the Charlie Gibson business?"

"He just got out of jail," Pappa explained. "Maybe…"

"What?" Dad cut him off. "That kid was in jail? How do you know that?"

Dad seemed about to burst.

"Have you been talking to that kid, Meera?"

"No!" I said, putting my arms up.

I wasn't lying. Leo hadn't been reachable by phone all this time.

"He's her latest project," Jeet butted in. "She's talking to all kinds of people for that kid."

Sally put a hand on Dad's arm. Some kind of magic juice must have flowed into him. I saw him almost shake with rage but he didn't say a thing.

I was more worried about what Leo wanted. Had there been a break in the case? Or had they arrested him again?

I held the phone up in the air and waved my arm to and fro, trying to catch a signal. A bar appeared for a fraction of a second. I pressed dial but I lost it again. Another missed call notification had come through in that time.

"Why is Leo trying to contact me now?" I wondered out loud.

My tension made me forget everything else.

"He should have reached Sylvie's by now," Motee Ba said.

"I'll call the diner," I said.

Then I remembered there was no way to do it.

"Maybe you'll get a signal at Hopi Point," Motee Ba offered.

Dad was silent all this time. It was a sign he was really mad at me. I would have to deal with him later.

We finally reached the parking area for the sunset point and scrambled out.

"It's just 4:45PM, Andy. Lots of time for sunset."

Dad pointed toward the crowds already thronging the spot. People sat along any vantage points, or stood at the railing. There didn't seem to be any empty spots closer to the edge.

"We can enjoy the sunset from right here," Motee Ba reasoned.

"Let's walk over there, Granny," Tony smiled, taking her arm. "We'll try to squeeze in."

"We'll get our turn," Pappa said, tapping his cane.

I lagged behind a couple of steps as everyone started walking to the summit. I flipped Tony's phone open and waved my arm around once again, trying to get the phone to connect. I switched hands, restarted the phone, popped open the battery and slid it in again, and finally banged the phone against my leg in frustration.

"No use! There's no signal here!" A guy told me as he walked across, waving his own phone in the air.

The girl with him gave him a quelling look. The guy sighed and put the phone in his pocket.

"Might as well enjoy the view," he told me as he walked away.

We reached the railings and a couple of people moved, making room at the railing. Pappa and Motee Ba clutched it and thanked them. Now we could take turns and each get the full 270 degree view of the sun setting across the valley.

Dad looked around, trying to gather our group close. His eyes bulged when he saw me staring at the phone screen.

"Do you have no shame?" he said coldly. "Put that phone away or I swear I'll toss it down there."

"It's Tony's phone!"

Sally pulled Dad away from me and pointed to something over the horizon. Tony crossed his arm and gave me a look loaded with disappointment.

I finally gave in and slapped the phone into his hand.

The sky had darkened a bit and the sun was emitting its last few rays before going down. A rainbow split the sky and a gasp went across the crowd. People were taking pictures like crazy. Tony was taking a video, and Jeet was asking the grownups to pose for photos. A deep orange glow shone over us, and shadows played along the canyon ridges, creating a new picture every minute. The sky was a flaming canvas of orange, pink, mauve and every color in between. I felt my heartbeat slow as I took in everything. My mind cleared of every thought as the blood orange orb of the sun gradually sank out of sight.

Sally took my hand and pulled me close. Jeet had asked another tourist to take a group photo of all of us. We smiled at the camera and I realized I was grinning ear to ear.

Tony took more pictures of the Patel clan. Dad and Sally posed, and Dad asked for a picture with Sally, Jeet and me. Then Tony and I posed together.

"That's enough," Pappa said finally, tapping his cane. "Let's get going."

We turned around for a final glimpse of the canyon. No one wanted to leave. The air had turned chilly and we were shivering in our jackets. Everyone wanted something hot to drink so Tony drove to the Grand Canyon Village. We still had an important task ahead – shopping.

After adding t-shirts, caps, shot glasses, fridge magnets and other sundry items portraying the Grand Canyon to our shopping cart, and a considerable dent in Dad's credit card, we finally started the drive back to the hotel. I had quietly picked out a T-shirt for Leo. He needed something to cheer him up after the ordeal he had been through.

We grabbed some munchies from the market and sipped hot coffee. Everyone was ready for a hot meal by the time we reached the town of Williams. We chose to have dinner at the hotel's restaurant again. This gave us a chance to freshen up a bit.

I had completely forgotten the phone and the missed calls. Dad was purposely ignoring me but I hardly noticed. He's preoccupied most of the time anyway. And he is also mad at me for some reason or the other.

I had ordered a traditional dinner with potatoes and vegetables. The creamy mash was heavy enough to make me drowsy. A fresh lemon meringue pie called to me and I wasn't about to ignore it.

"Please tell me we're not waking up at the crack of dawn tomorrow!"

We were back at the hotel, standing outside our room.

"Your Dad said we'll meet for breakfast at 9:30," Motee Ba assured me.

Everyone heaved a sigh of relief.

I collapsed on my bed and dozed off, too tired to think of anything. Tony was shaking me awake the next instant.

"Meera, wake up!"

"What is it? Is it morning already?"

I tried to force my eyes open. The room was dark except for a small bedside lamp and the flickering lights from the TV. Jeet was fast asleep. Tony was waving his phone in front of me.

"There's a bunch of missed calls here. I thought you might want to check them out."

The clock read 11 PM. I went into the bathroom and splashed some water on my face. I walked to the vending machine in the hallway and got a can of soda. The cold fizz was refreshing. I seemed to get a second wind after the short nap.

Back in the room, I stared at the list of calls I had missed. Many of them were from Leo. Why was he so desperate to get in touch?

I dialed the number in anticipation and crossed my fingers. There was no response. I redialed after waiting a couple of minutes.

I looked up at Tony, shaking my head.

"Must be asleep by now, Meera. They are an hour ahead of us."

I hoped that's all it was. Why else would Leo not answer my phone?

Chapter 17

"Do you think he's alright?" I couldn't hide the fear in my voice.

"Of course he is. What about the other calls?"

Tony pointed at his phone. It seemed like the whole world had wanted to talk to me.

"Some are from Stan, and some are from Becky. One of these is Sylvie's home number."

"So maybe Leo forgot something, then he called from Sylvie's place to let you know he was fine."

That was one reasonable explanation, but there could be so many more.

"What about Becky?"

"Didn't you ask her to talk to people? She's just checking in."

"It's too late to call her back, I guess."

The phone rang just then, startling us. It was Stan.

"Where have you been, Meera?" he said gruffly.

It looked like Stan wasn't getting much sleep either.

"The phone was out of range. What's the matter, Stan? Looks like you called. More than once."

"I've been working on some of your leads," he said.

Based on his tone, I didn't think he had any good news.

"I checked with Charlie's bank. He withdrew his usual 100 dollars last Wednesday. So nothing out of the ordinary there."

There wasn't any question of how Leo got hold of the money.

"About Don Collins," Stan sighed. "He was having dinner with his mother that evening. And then they watched TV."

"So they are each other's alibi? That's convenient."

"And she insists she saw Leo running away."

"Is that enough to put Leo in jail?"

"Things don't look good for the boy, Meera. His finger prints are on the knife. A witness claims he was seen escaping from the crime scene. And no one else will speak up for him. By the way, I checked the lights. There's a motion detector there, with a floodlight attached to it."

"What if someone came forth saying they spotted Anna elsewhere at that time?"

"That's just wishful thinking. What if one more person says they saw Leo jumping out of the window?"

"Have you talked to any more neighbors?"

"I didn't get to it today," Stan admitted. "I know you're taking this hard, Meera. But try to prepare yourself. Your boy's beginning to look guilty as hell."

I was speechless. Stan hung up, promising to keep me posted on the latest. I put my head on Tony's shoulder, trying to gather my thoughts.

"What do you know about him, really?" Tony asked gently.

"Pappa had his doubts. So does Dad, apparently. Sylvie, Motee Ba and I are the only ones who think Leo's innocent."

Tony gave me a meaningful look.

"What are you saying, Tony Sinclair? You think we are sentimental fools?"

His eyes softened and he hugged me close.

"You have a big heart, Meera. It's one thing I really love about you. But you can be too kind."

"I don't care what you say."

I really wanted to call Becky. Maybe she had found out something that would help Leo. I convinced myself to wait until morning.

Tony had warned me not to wake him up until 8:30. He also hinted I should switch off the phone's ringer. I fell asleep before I could count to 5 and woke up under a barrage of pillows. Jeet and Tony towered over my bed, ready to strike some more blows. A shrill sound finally penetrated my sleep deprived brain. It was the phone.

Tony pointed his arm toward the door.

I took the phone and went into the bathroom. It was Becky.

"What's up Becks? Everything alright?"

"Sure, Meera! It's almost 7 AM. I'm just starting my shift."

I bit back a curse. No wonder Tony and Jeet were mad at me.

"We didn't get a chance to talk yesterday," Becky was saying. "I thought we'd catch up before I get busy."

I told her about the Grand Canyon sunset.

"I'm missing all the fun, Meera. But I'm glad I stayed back. Sylvie hasn't been feeling too good."

"What's wrong?"

"She was running a slight fever yesterday. I told her not to rush in today. And I told Jon to stay back and take care of her."

"That's good of you, Becky!"

"It's the least I can do. Never mind all that. Wait till you hear what happened yesterday."

"Did you meet Leo?"

"Not yet. He wasn't home when I went by Charlie's."

"Did you get to talk to anyone this time?"

"You bet! Joyce Baker. Another of Charlie's neighbors."

"Who is she?"

"She's a sweet old lady with a house at the edge of the cul de sac. Her living room window has a great view of Charlie's house."

"Where was she all this time?"

"Right there. No one went to talk to her."

"Is she the one with the twitching curtains?"

"That's her. Sylvie says she's nosy. And a big gossip."

"That's good for us, right? But is she accurate or does she just spread tall tales?"

"How would I know that, Meera?"

"What did she tell you?"

Would she have something nice to say about Leo? Becky almost read my mind.

"She was all praise for Leo. He's as meticulous as Charlie. Does his chores right on time. Goes to the library every day too."

"Did Charlie talk to this woman?"

"I'm not sure. I guess she just observed all this from that window of hers. She told me Leo was a good kid. Then she turned red when I asked about Anna Collins. She said she wasn't feeling too good. So I had to leave."

"Why would she do that?" I cried.

"I don't know Meera," Becky was thoughtful. "It's almost as if she wants to say something about the Collins duo but doesn't dare to. Who knows? Maybe that Don guy's threatened her?"

"There's a good chance of that, based on his record. What else did she talk about?"

"More of the same stuff you know. Charlie was very particular about his routine. He waved to her every time he took Bandit out for a walk. But he didn't stop and chat with her."

"I'll ask Stan to go talk to her. Do you think she's hiding something?"

"Doesn't seem the type," Becky said. "She seemed eager enough to talk. Just clammed up when I mentioned Anna."

Becky hung up after that and I pulled out the index card with the question mark. I wrote down Joyce Baker's name and added a reminder to send Stan over to talk to her.

It was barely 6:30 but I couldn't sleep. I showered and dressed and decided to go on a drive. I left a note for the boys, just in case they woke up before I got back. I took the road to the canyon and put the car in cruise mode at 50 miles per hour. I didn't plan to drive as far as the park. I was hoping the drive would clear my head. The sun slowly came up on my right. I parked in a small clearing and rolled the windows down, breathing in the moist, cool air.

My life had grown complicated in the last few months. Simple moments like these had become elusive. I enjoyed the solitude, thinking about nothing for a change. The cold air began to make me drowsy and I finally made a U turn back to the hotel.

The boys were still fast asleep and I took great pleasure in waking them up.

"You didn't get us anything?" Jeet sulked.

I handed over two cups of coffee and popped the last bite of donut in my mouth. I wasn't in a mood to share.

"Breakfast in 30 minutes!"

"Did you sleep well?" I asked Pappa as I cut into my three egg omelet.

I was getting used to these lavish breakfasts. Any meal I don't have to cook is good enough for me. I savored the cheesy omelet with ham and green peppers, trying to ignore Dad who sat right opposite me at the table.

Sally placed a big bowl of fruit in front of him. He speared a piece of melon with gusto and beamed at her.

"Are you boys ready for our next stop?" Dad asked.

Jeet and Tony were grinning foolishly, thinking of Vegas showgirls.

"Just think about it. We'll go hundreds of feet down inside, and see the turbines spin."

I guffawed, spraying Dad with the contents of my mouth.

"He's talking about the dam, you bozos!"

"What's this nonsense, Meera?" Dad growled, wiping his face with a napkin Sally handed him.

"Sorry, Dad! This is just too funny. The boys are dreaming of naked girls and you're talking about boring old machines."

"She's lying!" Jeet protested, turning red in the face. "We're thinking of no such thing."

"Speak for yourself," Tony said under his breath.

"Don't you dare take my baby to that kind of place!" Motee Ba rapped Tony on the shoulder.

"Motee Ba," Jeet turned to her. "I'm over 18! I'm going to college!"

"Let's see the dam first," Dad said, hiding a smile. "We'll talk about what to do in Vegas when we get there."

All three women at the table glared at the men. Pappa finally looked up and realized he had missed something.

"What's going on, Hansa?"

"You should book a day at the spa with your mother," Dad said to me.

He turned to look at his mother.

"You should all go. My treat."

"That's a great idea," Motee Ba said and winked at me.

I didn't know how I felt about doing anything with Sally.

"Do you like going to spas?" I asked her.

She seemed well preserved for her age. Her skin was flawless, smooth and without any blemish. Some of it was genetics, but she had taken care of herself over the years. Sally Rossi exuded the kind of charm and class that came with wealth. I was sure she hadn't been picking oranges in California.

Sally gave me a smile. It meant she would love spending a day at the spa with me.

We lingered over the breakfast table. The next stop was Las Vegas, a three hour drive. Our hotel didn't allow check-ins until 3 PM. Even with an hour or two at the Hoover Dam, the day was wide open.

Pappa asked about lunch plans and everyone pitched in with ideas. Sally suggested getting bread and cheese from the market and making sandwiches. We still had some chilies and tomatoes left over from the farmer's market. Dad wanted to get something to go so Sally wouldn't have to exert herself making the sandwiches.

My phone rang, or rather Tony's phone rang. I got up from the table and walked a few steps away to answer it.

"Stan! I was going to call you after breakfast. We are just finishing up."

Stan's voice crackled over the lines, knocking the wind out of my sails. Tony's phone slipped from my hands and shattered on the terracotta tiles of the restaurant. I heard a buzzing sound in my ears. I saw Tony spring up from his chair and rush around to hold me. I must have struggled because his grip tightened. Then I was burying myself into his arms, trying to forget what I had just heard.

Chapter 18

Motee Ba stroked my back gently, and Sally sat next to me with my hand in hers. Pappa sat in a chair tapping his cane. The boys sat on the floor in a corner, quiet for once. Dad paced the room restlessly, muttering to himself.

We were all in Sally's room, trying to process what I had just heard.

Stan's voice rang in my ears and it still didn't make sense.

"Brace yourself, Meera," he had started. "The news is not good."

He had paused, as if taking a big gulp.

"They found Leo Smith this morning. He's gone. Took an overdose of sleeping pills."

I had heard nothing beyond that. Leo's face swam before my eyes. I was never going to see him again.

"Call Stan and get the details," Motee Ba ordered Tony.

"My phone's broken, Granny," Tony said.

"Borrow Andy's phone."

Dad stopped his manic pacing and stared at his mother.

"Really, Ba? Haven't we had enough of this? Good riddance, I say."

"Dad!" I cried.

Sally frowned and clutched my hand tighter.

"Don't be unkind, Andy," Motee Ba glared. "He never did anything to you."

"We need to know what happened," Pappa spoke up. "I promised Charlie I would keep an eye on that boy."

Dad reluctantly handed over his phone to Tony. I don't know how but Tony finally managed to get Stan on the line. He asked a couple of questions and then listened quietly for a long time. Then he thanked Stan and hung up, promising to keep in touch.

He stared at me, looking helpless. I could tell something unpleasant was coming up.

"Well?" Dad said curtly. "Speak up, Tony. We are waiting."

"Audrey found Leo this morning. She heard Leo got out of jail. She went to Charlie's house to clean and cook for him, like always. Leo was already dead."

There was a stunned silence.

"He took a bunch of sleeping pills," Tony added.

"So he didn't go to Sylvie's?" I croaked.

I hadn't had a chance to talk to Sylvie. Then I remembered she was sick. Maybe she had forgotten all about inviting Leo to her house.

"There's more," Tony almost whispered.

"What is it, dear?" Motee Ba asked gently.

"Leo left a note. He owned up to killing Charlie in a fit of anger. He said he was sorry, but he couldn't take it anymore. He was the only one to blame for Charlie's murder."

There was a collective gasp.

I was so shocked I couldn't utter a single word.

Dad banged a desk, a queer gleam in his eyes.

"That's it," he roared, looking around at everyone. "We have had enough of Charlie Gibson and that kid. No one will say a single word about him again. Chapter closed."

He gave me an intense look, daring me to protest. I didn't have an ounce of energy to say, do or feel anything.

"Pack up, kids," Dad ordered. "We hit the road in half an hour. Let's hope we all learned a lesson today."

His barb was directed at me but I didn't care.

We walked back to our room and I began stuffing my clothes in my bag.

"Let me do that, Meera."

Tony took me by the shoulders and coaxed me into a chair. Jeet brought a cold can of soda from the vending machine.

"Do you need some of Pappa's brandy?" he asked. "I can go get some."

I smiled at him weakly and shook my head.

"He called me so many times yesterday," I wailed.

"You think he wanted to confess?" Tony asked kindly.

"I don't know. Whatever it was, we could have sorted it out. If only he had told me what he was thinking, Tony…"

"You did all you could, Meera."

"Did I?" I cried. "I don't think so. I didn't return his call. I could have sent Becky over to talk to him, or Stan. I could have called a helpline."

"It wasn't meant to be," Tony droned.

"How can you be so cold, Tony? This is a kid we're talking about. A seventeen year old kid who was all alone in this world."

"He knew you cared about him, Meera. Didn't you tell him he could stay with you in the fall?"

Tony was just trying to make me feel better. But his words struck a chord.

"That's right. We discussed his future. He was upbeat. He was grieving over Charlie but he sounded positive. He was just going to get his stuff and go to Sylvie's."

"Looks like he was bluffing."

"I'm sure he wasn't," I said firmly. "Something happened since the time I talked to him yesterday morning. What do you think changed, Tony?"

All Tony could offer was a shrug.

"You need to dial it down, Meera. Uncle Andy won't tolerate any more talk about Leo."

"I need to talk to Stan, Tony," I said, grabbing his arm.

"Sorry, Meera. I can't help you there. My cell phone's broken. You need a calling card for long distance."

"I don't have one," I murmured.

"We'll have to wait until you can get one, then."

I thought about all the question marks I had on my index cards.

"We still have plenty of outstanding questions," I insisted. "How can the police be sure Leo really murdered Charlie?"

"A dying confession is generally considered to be the truth, Meera."

I shook my head. A lot of things did not add up. But I didn't know the whole story and I didn't have a way to talk to Stan. I didn't have a choice but to fall in line with Dad's wishes.

"I suppose you are happy now," I accused Tony. "I turned out to be the sentimental fool, just like you said."

Tony took my hands in his and stared into my eyes.

"I am not happy, Meera. Not at this price. I'd give anything to be wrong about this."

There was a knock on the door and Motee Ba came in. Her eyes were red and swollen and I realized she had been crying. I hadn't shed a single tear until then but I felt my eyes fill up. She hugged me close and we sobbed together, mourning a life that was taken from us too soon, without warning.

There are times like these when I wonder if God really exists.

"At least he won't suffer any more," Motee Ba said.

I didn't know what suffering she was talking about. Surely being alive, however poor or alone, is better than losing your life? But what do I know.

"Do you think like all these people, Motee Ba?" I asked, agonized. "Do you believe Leo could harm Charlie?"

Motee Ba suddenly looked old and frail.

"All this time, I believed he was a good kid, Meera. I thought people were being unfair to him because he was alone in this world. All I saw was a child who had no one to call his own, who needed a guiding hand like any other boy his age."

"Yes, yes."

"I was thinking with my heart, sweetie. I know nothing of the ways of the world. I am just an old woman who raises kids."

"You're much more than that, Motee Ba. You raised Dad and his siblings, and you raised us! You can read a person, know what he's thinking deep down."

"That's what I thought," Motee Ba said slowly. "But I don't know."

I stared at my grandmother, shocked by the defeat in her voice. She's the rock I have leaned on all my life. If my grandmother wasn't sure about a thing, how could I be sure?

"Don't say that, Motee Ba," I sobbed. "We were right. Leo Smith was a good person. I'm going to prove it."

Motee Ba looked uncertain.

"Your Dad is really angry about this, Meera. You can't do anything that will disturb him more."

"So you also think I should give this up?"

Her silence was answer enough.

"We've had our share of problems, haven't we, Meera? Your father wants to show you a good time. It's important to him. Let him do it, please."

"How can I smile and party when my heart wants to grieve?"

"You don't have a choice," she said flatly. "Put on an act if you have to. That's an order."

"Does Sally think Leo was a bad one? Is that why Dad is so convinced?"

"Don't drag your mother into this, Meera," Motee Ba said sharply. "She's having a hard time as it is."

"She's having a hard time?" I asked incredulously. "All she's doing is holding hands with Dad, singing songs, and cracking a smile once in a while."

"She's cooped up in a car with a bunch of strangers. Strangers who keep expecting her to remember something or the other, speak in a language she doesn't know, and expect fantastic things from her. Not to mention some people who judge her every minute."

"That's one way of looking at it!"

I rolled my eyes. Just thinking about Sally reminded me of how ridiculous my own life was.

"Wash your face and get ready. We don't want to be late."

I went into the bathroom and blew my nose. Motee Ba is always my silent supporter. Losing her as an ally shook my confidence. It looked like I would have to bow down to Dad after all.

"It's just for a few days," Tony tried to console me when I came out. "You can dig into this once we get back to Swan Creek."

He took my arm and led me out to the car. Jeet had already taken our bags out and loaded the car.

"I can drive now," Jeet was telling Dad.

"Maybe later," Dad said, getting behind the wheel.

I stooped and shuffled into the third row, a blank expression on my face. I would stay quiet about Leo, but I wouldn't be jumping with joy.

Even Dad couldn't expect me to be so callous, could he?

Chapter 19

Dad stuck to the speed limit on I-40 West but the car still ate up the miles. No one spoke for some time. Then Motee Ba began with some small talk, trying to get everyone to answer her. She's very good at this.

Sally joined in. It's amazing how she never misses an opportunity to suck up to Motee Ba.

I needed something to munch on and I needed Doritos. The ones that are smothered in that orange dust. We stopped somewhere and I jumped out without giving anyone a second glance. I wanted those chips and I wanted a calling card. They weren't selling any.

Stress eating is a boon. A bag of chips or a tub of ice cream can give me temporary amnesia when I desperately crave it. I sat at a picnic bench, expending all my angst on the chips.

"Don't bust a molar," Tony said lightly, dropping down on the seat beside me.

"Where did he get the sleeping pills?" I asked, buoyed by the sudden insight from a salt and carb rush.

"Did he have a prescription for insomnia? Did Charlie? Hunh? Did anyone check on that?"

Tony shook his head and stared at some point on the horizon.

"You need to wipe your face," he said.

So that's how it was going to be. I didn't want to pull out my index cards in front of everyone. But I made a mental note to myself.

"Are we still in Arizona?" Jeet asked, looking at a map.

"Of course we are still in Arizona, Jeet. Where do you think the state border is?"

Dad had found a new target for his anger.

"I don't know," Jeet said, sounding bored, and looked out of the window.

"Don't they teach you anything at school?"

No one answered that. Dad wasn't done.

"Maybe the question is don't you learn anything at school?"

Sally looked at Dad, trying to catch his eye.

"The state border is at the Hoover Dam!" Dad raised his voice in frustration. "It straddles Arizona and Nevada."

"Whatever!" Jeet said in a tone only a teenager can produce.

Silence reigned for a few more minutes.

"What about lunch?" Pappa asked.

He looked at his old watch and frowned. Pappa always frowns when he looks at his watch, no matter what the time is. He does things by the clock even though he hardly ever goes anywhere.

Amidst all the chaos, we had skipped going to the supermarket for sandwich fixings. We had also forgotten to pack lunch. We had worked through most of the snacks we had brought with us.

"We'll stop somewhere, Pappa!" Dad dismissed.

"But where?" Pappa wasn't one to concede the floor easily. "That's what I want to know."

We spotted signs for a diner and Dad pulled in there some time later. I didn't have much of an appetite. There wasn't much on offer anyway. Someone ordered a chicken sandwich for me and Motee Ba forced me to eat it.

They weren't offering the tour for the dam that day due to some technical reasons. Dad was going to sulk the rest of the day. We stood on the line between the two states and took pictures.

"You're in two places at once!" Tony exclaimed, reminding me of a movie we had watched together a few years ago.

The Hoover Dam is so vast, we were all speechless for a while.

We stood at the railing and gazed down at the humungous wall of the dam, and the still waters of Lake Mead. The Colorado river snaked it's way deep down somewhere on the other side.

I walked along a small sidewalk, lost in thought. Something flashed before my eyes for an instant. I searched around and spotted a familiar sight. It had been etched into the wall, and I wondered why. I looked around for Tony and tipped my head, calling him by my side.

"Do you see that?" I asked, pointing to the small doodle.

"What?"

"That right there, that doodle etched into the wall."

"That triangle like thing?" Tony asked.

He gave me a look. It said I was losing it.

"What about it Meera?"

"Do you think it's related to those other symbols I showed you?"

"I don't think so," he said flatly, and turned away.

"Maybe there are more of these around here," I pleaded, clutching his arm.

"Time to go, I think."

Dad was waving his arms, summoning the family to the car.

I skimmed the wall rapidly, and the sidewalks and any other structures I could spot around me. The small doodles were part of a puzzle, I was sure. They had to mean something, and I wanted to know what.

Dad asked Tony to drive and sat next to him. I was squashed into the back with Sally and Jeet.

"How are you doing today, Mom?" Jeet asked, leaning into her.

She smiled.

"Aren't you excited about going to Vegas?"

Sally produced one more smile, the kind that said yes.

I looked out of the window at the cars passing by. I noticed something on a car window and it reminded me of my doodles. There wasn't much traffic and I tried to build different scenarios of what the drawings might represent. It distracted me from the real things on my mind.

I got tired of looking at cars after a while and my thoughts drifted to Leo. Had he spoken to Sylvie at all yesterday? Why hadn't he gone to her place with his stuff? Maybe he had never had any intention of going there. But he had told me he would. Was that a lie?

Only Sylvie could tell me if she had talked with Leo. I didn't know how sick she was. If she had something contagious, she might have asked Leo to stay put at Charlie's for a day or two.

I also wondered about Joyce Baker. Did that old lady know something? Or was she just trying to grab attention? Lonely people often do that. Show they know more than they do, so people go and talk to them again and again.

I just hoped I would remember all this until I had a chance to note it down.

The excitement in the car was contagious. We entered the city of Las Vegas, Nevada and every face broke into a smile. Dad entered the downtown area and merged onto Las Vegas Boulevard, the famous Strip. We craned our necks to look up at the Stratosphere Casino. It shot up into the sky, promising unforgettable views.

"We're going to the top and doing that ride," Jeet exhaled.

Tony and Jeet had talked endlessly about a ride at the top of the Stratosphere. You took a deep vertical plunge and were suspended mid air, hundreds of feet above the Las Vegas skyline.

We passed Circus Circus and The Mirage and Dad was pulling into our hotel lobby. Dad had splurged for rooms at the Bellagio, one of the pricier hotels on the Strip.

"Can we see those fountains from here?" Pappa asked Motee Ba. "We'll see them at least twice, Hansa. Once in daylight and once at night."

Jeet was staring wide eyed at a massive Eiffel Tower replica on the other side of the street. People of all ages and ethnicities milled around. Old men and babies in strollers shared sidewalk space. Cabs rolled into the hotel's porte cochere in rapid succession. Dad ordered us to help with the bags. There were bellboys around, but we had a lot of bags.

"We are on the same floor," Dad said, handing out room keys after we had finished checking in.

"Your room faces the fountains, Pappa. You can watch them all you want."

He turned toward us and spoke to Tony.

"Your room is pool facing. But I'm not sure if the pools are open at this time."

The elevator whisked us up to the 29th floor and I felt a smidgen of anticipation. The view from the higher floors was going to be fantastic. I had never stayed in a room that high up.

We burst into our room as soon as Tony swiped the key card. Our mouths dropped open. The room was huge and done in soothing colors. It was as lavish as I had imagined. No money had been spared in decorating it.

The bathroom had a spa tub with jets, the TV was huge and the mini bar was stocked with plenty of snacks.

I wanted to get away from it all.

I emptied some colorful bottles that lined the tub. I banged the door shut in the boys' face before they could say a thing. Opening the taps wide, I drowned out their voices, flinging my clothes off. Slowly, I let myself sink into the tub, hardly feeling the hot water burn my skin.

The tears started flowing again and I succumbed. Judging by

Dad's mood, he would probably forbid me from crying. I couldn't figure out why he was being so unfair. The lavender and lemon scented water began to soothe me and I almost fell asleep in the tub.

"Are you okay?" Tony's gentle voice sounded outside the door.

"I'm fine! Go away!"

Tony generally has my back. But he had seemed to agree with Dad today. Was he just trying to keep the peace, or did he really think I was being foolish?

"We're going down to get a snack," Jeet yelled.

The door slammed behind them. I sighed with relief. I showered and wrapped myself in a fluffy robe. It was soft and thick, and any other day I would have snuggled into it with joy. Today wasn't that day.

I looked forward to a long quiet nap. Maybe I wouldn't wake up until tomorrow. I grabbed the tiny bottle of moisturizer from the marble counter and opened the door. Tony leaned against the wall, arms folded, waiting for me.

"What're you doing here?" my mouth twisted in a grim line.

"You didn't think I was going to abandon you?"

The tears started fresh and I made no effort to stop them. Tony opened his arms wide and I rushed in, feeling the pain of losing Leo all over again.

Chapter 20

When you're in Las Vegas, the real fun begins at night. Or that's what people say. I was about to discover that the excitement never let up in this city, whether it was day or night. Inside the casinos, there was no sense of time with the bright lights and the allure of hitting the jackpot. Old ladies lined the aisles of slot machines, feeding coins and yanking the levers. Their eyes swelled with anticipation one moment, and their shoulders slumped in another when the numbers didn't line up. Once in a while, someone at a table would win big and a cheer would go up.

Tony and I walked across the casino floor, taking it all in. He couldn't wait to try his luck.

"Let's grab a bite real quick," he urged, pulsing with excitement.

"You better hand over your cash and credit cards, cowboy!"

"Don't say you're not going to try your luck, Meera!"

I looked around, ignoring Tony, trying to spot some place to eat. We walked to what looked like a food court and I grabbed a table. A bowl of Lo Mein sounded good to me.

Motee Ba and Pappa had decided to rest. They would just go down once and see the fountains light up. But other than that, they were having an early night.

Dad and Sally were checking out the shows the hotel had to offer. Dad insisted we watch some circus, and Sally wanted to book our spa appointments.

I shoveled the hot noodles in, thinking about what I wanted to do. A young girl was refilling the paper napkins at the tables. I caught her eye and beckoned her.

"Where can I find a store that sells batteries?"

"You can get batteries at the small kiosk over there."

She pointed her finger somewhere in the distance. Her voice dropped a level.

"But they overcharge."

She giggled at her choice of words and I gave her a wan smile.

"There's a Wal-Mart a couple of miles away."

"Don't you have convenience stores? Smaller shops?"

"Hard to find on this section of the Strip," she shook her head. "You'll have to go downtown, or go away from the Strip to one of the gas stations."

I thanked her. Getting my hands on a calling card looked tough.

"We can go tomorrow," Tony said, guessing what I was up to. "I really don't want to head out again."

"I want to call Stan. I've already waited too long."

"Look, let's just stroll along the Strip. We just might find a small store somewhere."

My chances of hitting the jackpot sounded better.

Jeet joined us as we headed out.

"Where have you been? You can't go into the casinos, can you?"

He ignored me.

The Strip was lit up like a string of diamonds. There was a palpable excitement in the air. Casinos soared into the sky, each offering something unique to the visitors. The lights on the Eiffel Tower twinkled, and the fountains danced to classical music.

"It's beautiful!"

"Which way?" Tony asked.

"The pirates' show," Jeet said right away. "It's on every hour, I think. We'll just wait until the next one."

"That's North, toward downtown," Tony pointed.

I fell in line. My chances of finding a small store were better as we went closer to the heart of town. The pirate show was just beginning. We didn't get a spot near the water but it didn't matter much. The show was a blur for me. My thoughts strayed back home while my eyes scanned every spot on the street, trying to find a store. I spotted a man ripping open a pack of AA batteries.

"Where'd you get those?" I asked.

He pointed vaguely toward the downtown area.

"Let's watch this again," Jeet said wide eyed as the show ended.

I feigned boredom and started walking away. They fell in line. The crowd started thinning after a while and Tony moved closer to me.

"Maybe we should turn back."

I opened my mouth to protest and I saw a tiny cluster of stores up ahead. A souvenir shop butted against a sub shop which was right next to an electronics store. I rushed in and started hunting for calling cards.

"What kind of phone you looking for, lady?" the man at the counter asked.

"Actually, I want a calling card."

"Don't keep them anymore," he said. "Most people have them cell phones. What with nationwide calling and all, no one's using calling cards no more."

I gave him a brief nod and walked out. Tony and Jeet were trying on a bunch of baseball caps. And there, next to mugs and shot glasses on an adjoining shelf, I saw a sign for calling cards.

I bought a couple from the man at the counter and walked out.

"Hey Meera! Don't you want one?"

Jeet and Tony had bought matching Las Vegas T-shirts and had pulled them on over their clothes. Jeet was holding one out for me.

"You look like a silly tourist."

Jeet's face fell into a hurt expression.

"I am a silly tourist."

I shook my head and whirled around, eager to get back to my room. Tony paid up quickly and the boys followed, urging me to put the T-shirt on. I gave in, just to make them shut up. They put their arms around my shoulders and we walked arm in arm, the boys humming some silly song.

Until I came up short a few steps later. We almost stumbled and fell.

"What was that, Meera?" Jeet wailed.

I felt a shiver run up my spine. I pointed to the sidewalk, and stammered as I tried to get Tony's attention.

"What now?" he asked.

"Do you see that?"

There was a charcoal drawing on the sidewalk, roughly two feet by two feet.

"That wasn't there when we walked by earlier."

"So?" Tony raised his eyebrows.

"Don't you recognize it? It's from the photos."

Tony straightened and looked carefully.

"I didn't look at them that closely," he admitted.

"What are you guys talking about?" Jeet asked.

I explained how I had first noticed the doodles, and how we'd seen them around rest areas, gas stations, almost every place we stopped.

I didn't say anything about the cars I had noticed earlier today.

"Haven't you heard of graffiti, Meera?" Jeet asked. "Looks something like it."

"These are too small. And there's some kind of pattern here."

"We talked about this, Meera. So they're some kind of puzzle. Nothing to do with us."

"You're in enough trouble already," Jeet reminded me.

"But this wasn't here a few minutes ago!" I insisted.

"Someone drew it just for you, to make you think you're crazy."

"Thanks for that sarcasm, Tony."

We walked on, the boys signing to each other over my head. I bet they thought I was losing it.

"A good night's sleep is what we all need," Tony droned.

"Okay, grandpa!"

"We've been on the move for six days now, Meera. I don't know about you, but I'm exhausted!"

"Hey, doesn't our hotel have room service?" Jeet asked with a wicked grin.

"How about some mac and cheese, hunh?" Tony asked, knowing I've never turned down a plate of cheesy pasta in my life.

"And a banana split!" Jeet added.

My mouth watered but I managed to keep a straight face.

It was late when we entered the hotel. The place was like a busy airport. Jeet turned me around and pointed toward something in the distance. Dad and Sally were framed in a restaurant window, having dinner. A glass of wine lay in front of both of them. Dad leaned forward, saying something. Sally looked down and blushed.

I grabbed Jeet and we went to the elevators. Tony had placed the room service order by the time I changed into my jammies.

"I'm sure Uncle Andy won't grudge us some food," he grinned wickedly.

There was a knock on the door a few minutes later and a uniformed man pushed in a trolley full of dishes, just like in the movies. There was a dome shaped lid over each of them. He pulled up each lid with a flourish, announcing the names of the dishes.

"Macaroni & cheese with truffles, cheeseburger, fish and chips…" he declared.

Tony and Jeet clapped their hands like kids. Tony smoothly slipped him a fiver and the man smiled.

"I'll bring your dessert in about thirty minutes."

The aroma of the food filled the room and even I couldn't resist. I took a bite of the steaming cheeseburger before Tony could say a thing.

"I'm not sharing!" I warned, as I picked up my pasta plate.

Jeet had found HBO on TV and an action movie was just about to start. Pasta had never tasted so good, nor had fish or meat, judging by the boy's reaction. The sundae the server brought in later was the largest I had ever seen, with six banana halves, about a dozen ice cream scoops and all kinds of toppings. There was a mountain of whipped cream on top of everything.

We dug into the ice cream and ate until we began to feel sick.

"It's too late to call anyone now," Tony whispered as I got up to sneak into the bathroom.

The wall clock showed midnight and I realized he was right.

"Who said I was calling anyone?"

"Why are you taking your bag into the bathroom?" Tony asked.

"It's girl stuff. You shouldn't ask me about such things, Tony. Bad manners."

"I've seen you buy 'girl stuff' plenty of times, Meera," Tony said, sounding irritated. "You think I don't know what you bought in that little shop? Why you made us walk all the way to the other end of the Strip?"

"So you know."

I noticed the dark circles under his eyes. Maybe Tony was right and we all needed some sleep.

"Let's tackle this tomorrow. Please."

"Why are you guys fighting?" Jeet called out in a sleepy voice.

I dumped my bag in the closet and collapsed on my bed. I was too full to sleep right away. Or so I thought.

I was out like a light the moment my back hit the mattress. A smiley face taunted me across the streets of Vegas, following me everywhere. It stopped as I entered a big bathroom and began chanting 'girl stuff' in a childish voice. More smiley faces appeared next to it, and they all started taunting me. I turned and fled, running in large strides across the Strip. A few minutes later, I hit a wall, or so I thought. I looked up to see a giant Stan Miller looming over me.

"End of the road," he said, waving a cell phone in front of me.

Chapter 21

I woke up well rested. Tony walked in with coffee and croissants. Jeet stirred and sat up in bed.

My coffee was perfect, with two sugars and just the right amount of cream. Melted chocolate oozed out of the croissant and I closed my eyes to savor the buttery, flaky pastry.

"Are we going to the breakfast buffet?" Jeet asked, wolfing down his croissant.

"You need to appreciate good food," I nagged.

"I took chai lattes to Granny's room," Tony said.

He had been up for a while, judging by his appearance. He smelt of the hotel soap instead of his usual Zest bar. Wet hair curled around his neck and I realized how much Tony was a fixture in my life. I missed some of what he was saying.

"So they'll meet us down there, and we can discuss the plans."

"What?"

"Wake up!" Tony said, tickling my feet as he sat on the edge of my bed.

"I want to hit at least 4-5 buffets while we're here," Jeet said. "For breakfast, lunch and dinner."

"Let's try the first one," Tony kidded.

The breakfast buffet was as lavish as the brochures said. Every kind of roll or baked item was on offer. There were live stations for pancakes, waffles and omelets. Quiches and frittatas vied for space with ordinary eggs and bacon. I put in an order for Eggs Benedict and lapped up the creamy Hollandaise sauce. I could have made a meal out of the different types of potatoes alone.

"Don't fill up on bread," Motee Ba said. "Have you tried the crepes?"

I had no idea how we were going to walk anywhere after all that food.

"I hope you've factored in a nap," I said to Dad as I let out a burp.

"We're going shopping," Motee Ba announced. "We all need a dress for tonight's show."

"For the circus?" I exclaimed.

"Are you really going to argue over this?" Motee Ba laughed.

I wasn't. Sally got up along with us and I realized she would tag along. She's got a good fashion sense so I decided I could use her.

We walked over to Caesar's, the adjoining casino. Sally said they had some good shops. The casino ceiling was made up of a blue sky with fluffy white clouds. It seemed so real my mouth dropped open. A show was going on somewhere and there were all kinds of stores set in a wide circle. I spotted big names. I had never been into these stores.

"Aren't these expensive?" I wondered.

Add two zeroes over my usual dress budget. Motee Ba pulled me along behind Sally and I discovered how rich people shop. They just point at stuff and try it on, without looking at the price tag. I got a couple of dresses, shoes made with the softest Italian leather, a matching bag and a bottle of expensive French perfume. There must be something to the concept of retail therapy. I was on a curious high when I went back to the room with all those packages. We were meeting for a light lunch in the Bellagio Café before going for our spa appointments.

I opened my bag to get the room key, a piece of plastic, really. I rifled through, shoving aside something stuffed in an envelope. I realized what it was as I dumped the bags on a couch and collapsed on my bed.

I had completely forgotten all about calling Stan.

I tore open the envelope and scratched the card for the PIN. Stan's phone connected almost instantly.

"Hello, Meera!" he said. "How are you?"

"I dropped my phone the other day and there was no way to call you."

Stan didn't need an explanation but I wanted him to know why I hadn't called since yesterday. Had it been just yesterday?

"The case is closed, Meera."

It was all over. That's what Stan meant.

"There's a lot of loose ends," I began. "Please, just hear me out."

"Go on!"

"Did you see the note Leo wrote?"

Stan grunted. I took that to mean yes.

"Are you sure it's his handwriting? What if someone else wrote the note?"

Stan cleared his throat but didn't say anything.

"How do you know he took an overdose?"

"Didn't Tony tell you?" Stan asked. "We found him slumped over the dining table with a half empty bottle of sleeping pills. The bottle was on top of the note."

"Did Leo have a prescription for those pills? Where did they come from all of a sudden?"

"They could have been Charlie's pills," Stan said.

"But were they? Who were they made out to? What did the prescription label say?"

Stan hadn't checked the label. But he wasn't ready to concede his mistake this time.

"It's not that hard to get some pills," he said, "even in a small town like Swan Creek, unfortunately. He could have got them from someplace else too. Didn't he just get back from a trip?"

"Are you saying Leo planned to take his own life even before Charlie died? How could he know Charlie was dead before he got back to Swan Creek?"

"Well, the theory is that he killed Charlie and went out of town. So he knew!"

"And he scored the pills for what? Taking his own life?"

"Maybe it was a backup plan? In case he was accused of murder?"

Stan had found a way to justify why Leo had those pills.

"You really think a young, innocent kid will take his own life?"

"That's the story, Meera," Stan said. "It's been written up in the papers. The news wires have picked it up, and it's spreading everywhere. Some are calling it a cautionary tale. They are saying it's best to stay away from troubled youth. Others are questioning the system, asking what the government is doing for these delinquents."

"Leo wasn't a delinquent!"

"Apparently he was. We finally ran him through the system."

I was beginning to lose my temper.

"He was a sweet kid. He was grieving for Charlie, but he was looking forward to life."

"What did he have to look forward to?" Stan smirked. "Living in some group home, sleeping on the streets, or worse?"

"No such thing, Stan. We were going to take care of him."

"How?"

"Sylvie was taking him in for a while. He was going to come live with us in the fall. He had a home until he went to college."

Stan paused. He hadn't seen this coming.

"That was mighty nice of you, Meera. Guess you Patels dodged a bullet there. You've got old people at home too."

I ignored what Stan was hinting at.

"Don't you see? I had already talked to Leo about all this. He had a bright future to look forward to. He was going to pack his bags and head over to Sylvie's."

"But he didn't!"

"Yes. Something happened between then and the time he died."

"He decided he couldn't live with the guilt," Stan said stonily. "That's what happened, Meera."

I sighed. Stan had made up his mind.

"Are you at least going to do an autopsy?"

"We'll follow the usual process, Meera."

That was a yes. I remembered Joyce Baker.

"One more thing. Do you know who Joyce Baker is?"

"Old lady," Stan said, trying to recollect. "A bit of a nosy parker, I think. Doesn't she live by Charlie's?"

"Becky talked to her. Looks like she knows Charlie's routine very well."

"She spends most of her time behind that curtain," Stan agreed. "There have been some complaints, but there's nothing we can do. She can do whatever she wants inside her house."

"Joyce Baker clammed up when Becky mentioned Anna Collins. I think she's afraid of her."

"Say she is. So what?"

"She's hiding something, Stan. I think it has to do with Anna or her son."

"Don's got a bad reputation, Meera. And he lives up to it. I bet everyone around that block looks the other way when they see Don."

"What if Anna or her son met Charlie the day he died? Or got into a fight?"

"You're just grasping at straws, Meera."

"Anna didn't get along with Charlie Gibson. She threatened to get even with him. Charlie put Don in jail. Maybe Don wanted revenge now that he's out on parole."

"So that he can go back in? Surely he's smarter than that?"

"He's a hardened criminal. That's what you said, Stan."

"The case is already closed, Meera. And there's no end to this speculation. Why don't you enjoy your trip? You'll be back soon enough. We can talk about this then."

"You're right, Stan," I murmured.

Stan Miller can be bull headed. It's hard to convince him of something he doesn't want to see. I might fare better face to face. We exchanged some small talk and I promised to get Stan something from Vegas.

"My room number's 2929 at the Bellagio, just in case."

I went into the bathroom, trying to hold back a fresh bout of tears. The bathroom fairy had visited in my absence. All the tiny bottles had been replenished, and arranged in a systematic order. I unwrapped the little soap, lost in thought. The cold water and the scented soap anchored me a little.

I went out and dialed the diner.

Sylvie answered. Her voice sounded hoarse. Was it from a cold or from a lot of crying?

"Hello Sylvie."

I had a sudden lump in my throat.

"Meera! How are you, child? How is your grandma?"

"As fine as can be, Sylvie, under the circumstances."

"They are saying he killed Charlie and took his own life." Sylvie cut to the chase. "But I don't believe it. We need you here, Meera."

"I just spoke to Stan," I told her. "They have closed the case."

There was silence at the other end.

"Hello? Hello?"

Becky's voice crackled across the line.

"She's crying," Becky said softly. "How are you taking this, Meera?"

"Not well," I admitted. "Dad doesn't want me to talk about it. He threw a fit yesterday. He said good riddance."

Becky gasped loudly. So she still believed me.

"Tony's on Dad's side too," I said grimly.

For me, it was the ultimate betrayal. I knew Becky would feel the same.

"It's all over the papers," Becky reported. "The Swan Creek Daily had a full front page story on it, and many of the bigger news papers have picked it up."

"Say you don't believe it, Becky!"

"Of course I don't. Wait, Sylvie wants to talk."

Sylvie came on the line again. Her voice sounded stronger.

"He called me from Charlie's house that day."

She was talking about Leo of course.

"Said Audrey was doing a load of laundry for him. He was coming to my place as soon as he packed a few clothes. I told him we were waiting."

"How did he sound?"

"He thanked me for inviting him. He sounded relieved, Meera. And happy. No way that child was thinking about ending it all."

"Did you call when he didn't turn up?"

"That's just it. I wasn't feeling too good. I took some aspirin and turned in early."

"Did you talk to Audrey after that?"

"I haven't seen her since then."

Was Audrey Jones involved in this mess? She had been on the scene the night Charlie died. And she was the one person who had access to the house. As private as Charlie was, Audrey must have been aware of his affairs. Maybe Audrey had done away with Charlie for some reason unknown to us. Leo could have confronted her about it. She could have easily poisoned Leo, then staged it to look like he took the pills.

I barely said goodbye to Sylvie. My mind was buzzing with all kinds of scenarios. There was a knock on the door. I smelt Sally's perfume mixed with Motee Ba's Chanel.

"Meera! You ready, sweetie?"

I let them in with a smile on my face.

"Just a minute, Motee Ba!"

I brushed my hair and freshened my lipstick and I was ready to go.

"Your mother's craving pizza," Motee Ba said. "Does that sound okay to you?"

Sally would probably eat one slice of pizza with a mound of salad. I would eat half a pie with more cheese on top. Stan's words haunted me and any kind of bread with hot melted cheese sounded good to me.

Chapter 22

I let myself be pummeled and pounded. It was therapeutic, I had to admit. Sweet and pungent fragrances from the oils and creams assailed my senses. I had no choice but to breathe in deeply. I found myself retreating to a zone where my mind wasn't capable of a single thought.

We beamed at each other after our massage and facials, dressed in fluffy ivory robes, letting our feet be rubbed. Motee Ba insisted we all choose the same nail color.

"This is the life!" she sighed happily. "I can't wait to tell Anita."

Anita is my aunt, Motee Ba's daughter. She's a pro at this kind of thing. I had a feeling Sally was going to offer good competition.

"I'm taking a nap after this," Motee Ba announced.

"There's so much to see," I reminded her.

Dad and the boys had gone to watch the sharks at the Mandalay Bay aquarium. They were starting at the top of the Strip and making their way down. I wanted to go on a gondola ride at the Venetian.

"Not today! Our show starts at 6 and we'll go to dinner after that."

I called Becky to dish about the spa.

"Audrey was here," she told me, "for lunch."

"So she's still spreading around the cash."

"Do you think she knows something about Charlie's will? He may have left her something for all her years of service."

"Where is this will, Becky? Why hasn't it surfaced yet?"

"Maybe she' got it. She's just waiting for some time before showing it to anyone. Or she doesn't know what to do with it."

I had a thought.

"What's wrong with asking her?"

"She might not like it," Becky warned.

"Just ask her about the will, not the other stuff. Ask her if Charlie ever talked about a will, or if she ever saw one in that house. That should get her talking if she knows anything."

I hung up and took a nap. Then it was time to get ready.

The bedside phone trilled. It was Motee Ba.

"Eat something before you get dressed. I am ordering room service."

That sounded like a good idea. I ordered sandwiches for us, knowing the boys would be hungry too. When are they not?

I relished the club sandwich and began to get dressed. I couldn't recognize myself in the mirror. Tony's eyes popped when I opened the door. Jeet laughed. There's something about pricey clothes alright. The dress fell in soft folds, clinging softly to my curves without looking tight. The shoes and the bag made me look like a person I'm not.

There was another knock on the door. Sally came in. She handed me a small velvet box. I opened it to find emerald ear rings.

"For me?"

She smiled.

"I can't accept these. They look expensive."

Sally smiled again and held the box out, refusing to retreat. Dad walked in and looked at me.

"Your mother wants you to wear them tonight, Meera."

Well, as long as they were just a loan. I didn't want anything from this woman. Certainly not something that was bought by her fake husband.

Dad glanced at me again and his face melted.

"You look beautiful."

The circus was something else. The exorbitant tickets were worth the price. So was all the dressing up. We all sat transfixed through the entire show. We had a dinner reservation after that and then we were all free to do what we wanted.

"We need to watch the fountains," I reminded Tony.

Imagine the irony if we didn't take in a single fountain show inspite of staying at the Bellagio. Everyone wanted to change first. I felt comfortable pulling on my jeans, but I missed the dress right away. The sidewalk was crowded even at 10 PM and people were craning their necks to get a good view. The day was just beginning in Las Vegas.

We tried our luck at some slots and won $10. Jeet stood at the other end of the room, away from the casino floor. Tony bought us ice cream after that.

"What do you think of Audrey Brown?" I asked Tony.

He frowned.

"Do you think she could do it, Tony?"

"Isn't the case closed now?"

I gave him a look.

"Of course! How can it be closed if Meera Patel suspects otherwise?"

I quailed at the sharp note in his voice. He was angry about something.

We checked out some Harleys in a hotel dedicated to them. Tony flagged a cab and we went to the Stratosphere. My ears pinged as the elevator took us to the top. I watched, terrified, as Jeet and Tony let themselves be suspended mid air. Leo would never have this kind of fun. He had never had a chance.

We entered a mall and walked a mile deep into it. I had to sit down to rest my feet. I grabbed a table at a café and ordered hot chocolate. Someone left an old newspaper at the table next to us and I picked it up.

"Guys, do you realize we have no idea what's going on in the world right now?"

Jeet rolled his eyes. When has a teenager cared about world peace? Dad must be watching the news headlines on TV every morning. But the TV in our room had never been tuned to anything other than movies.

It was a California paper from some coastal town, a name I recognized. I went to graduate school in California and my uncle lives in the Bay area. I have been to a lot of places in the state.

Leo's face was emblazoned across an inner page. He looked like he was sleeping. I gasped as I realized what that meant. Couldn't they have used his driver's license photo? Half the page was devoted to the story. It explained how Leo had cold bloodedly killed the hand that fed him. Charlie Gibson was mentioned. And then Leo's remorse and suicide was played up. The writer pointed out the tragedy behind the whole episode. The piece turned it into a big issue about providing proper care for orphans and homeless kids.

"This is not right," I fumed. "This is defamation."

"Has she found a new 'project'?" Jeet drawled.

I felt like socking him one. I have been known to do it too.

Tony peered across the table and tipped the paper down to read. He's good at reading things upside down. He sobered as the story sank in.

"This does seem to be the official version," he said slowly.

He wanted me to accept the truth and move on.

"You can't win 'em all, Meera. Anyone can make a mistake."

The clanging in my head began anew. I didn't know who to trust. Becky had said the story was spreading. And it had spread as far as California! It certainly looked like the authorities had no doubts about the chain of events.

A part of me still felt bad for Leo. Even if I convinced myself he was guilty of killing Charlie, I couldn't wrap my head around his suicide. It could have been easily avoided. Maybe Leo had pulled a knife on Charlie in a burst of emotion. Or maybe they fought over something. He could have lived out any sentence and resumed his life.

Death is so final. Why does anyone think it is necessary?

"You wanted this guy to come live in our home?" Jeet asked coldly.

He had read the story by this time.

"There's some mistake," I pleaded. "Surely Leo wasn't that bad?"

"You trusted him too much. That's the mistake." Jeet looked perplexed. "Why, Meera? Were you sweet on him?"

I clenched my fists under the table. Jeet was just being an obnoxious teen.

"Let's go," Tony said, getting up.

He wanted to trash the paper. I wasn't sure if I should keep it.

We walked back to the hotel. A smiley face on the sidewalk mocked me. I wasn't in a mood to solve any more mysteries. We convinced Jeet to go up to the room and headed toward the casino.

"Why don't you go on up?" Tony said to Jeet. "They'll ask you for ID anyway, bro."

Now Tony wanted to try his luck at the blackjack table. I was more interested in the drinks the skimpily dressed girls were carrying around on trays. One of the girls placed a frosty can in front of me, along with a paper napkin.

"Tough day?" she asked sympathetically.

I thanked her and tried to follow the game on the table. Tony won a couple of times and then he was on a losing streak. He lost all his chips, and he stood up, laughing.

"That was fun!"

"You just lost fifty dollars, champ!"

"Yeah! But now I can say I played Blackjack at the Bellagio in Las Vegas. Some things you just do for the experience, kid."

I couldn't help but smile.

"What else is on that list for Las Vegas?" I teased.

Tony winked and said nothing. I didn't really want to know anyway.

We went up to our room, ready to turn in. Tony was out within minutes. I was wide awake. I rifled though my bag, looking for my secret stash of candy. I came across the index cards. I looked through them one by one, remembering all the questions I had raised over the last week. Some of them were not applicable any more, or were already resolved. I took a pencil and drew a line through those.

Then I thought of Bandit. I had completely forgotten him. Joyce Baker had mentioned Charlie walked him every evening. Audrey or Leo had said he let Bandit out at 8 PM one last time. Had he let the dog out at 8 PM? That would establish if Charlie was still alive at 8. If he was, then Anna Collins was definitely lying.

Two questions had still not been resolved to my satisfaction.

Where did Audrey get so much money all of a sudden? Why was Anna Collins lying? I realized there was one more question no one had raised. Why did Bandit not bark at the intruder? And where had the dog been when Charlie was stabbed.

Stan would rule out these points. He would dismiss my concerns against Anna or Audrey as mere speculation. He would say the dig didn't bark because he knew the person who killed Charlie. It was someone who lived in the house.

Every argument that applied to Leo also applied to Audrey Jones. I needed to shake her down. But I would have to wait until I got back to Swan Creek. Unless Becky managed to ask her some tough questions.

Chapter 23

I woke up to an empty room again. One of the boys had thrust the drapes wide open. The room was bathed in silvery sunlight and I crinkled my eyes. They had let me sleep in.

There was a note on the table, asking me to get ready and come to Motee Ba's room. I took my time since no one seemed to be in a hurry. What a relief that was, after a week of being rushed off my feet. I dressed in layers as usual and knocked on Motee Ba's door, craving a cup of coffee.

The mild buzz inside meant some live discussion was going on.

Everyone had a cup of something in their hands. Motee Ba poured a cup for me from a flask. It wasn't too hot and I made a face.

"You can have more at breakfast."

"Where are we eating today?" Jeet asked.

Dad and Sally were seated at the edge of the bed. Pappa was ensconced in an arm chair with his feet up on the ottoman. Dad held up a flyer and called for attention.

"We are going on a drive. So no buffet this morning."

"You can drive to wherever you want," Pappa declared. "But I am having lunch at this Indian restaurant."

He produced his own flyer, some kind of coupon for a lunch buffet. It's a marvel Pappa had gone without Indian food for so long.

"We may not be back in time for that," Dad said.

Pappa looked disappointed.

"Unless," Dad said, looking around, "we grab breakfast at some drive through."

Everyone seemed fine with that. We agreed to meet in the lobby in 30 minutes. I went to my room to get my stuff.

Since I was already dressed, I called Becky.

"When do you get back, Meera?" she sounded gloomy.

I told her about the newspaper I found.

"You don't say! That must have been a shock."

I mentioned the photo.

"What's wrong with these people? How could they share that kind of photo with the press?"

I shuffled my index cards as I talked to Becky.

"So these questions are still outstanding. Maybe you can ask Audrey? Or go meet Joyce Baker again? The police have closed the case."

"Audrey might come in here," Becky said. "She's making a habit of it."

"Have you heard of anyone else hiring her?"

"She's not looking for work yet," Becky said. "She's taking some time off."

"Maybe she saved up some money working for Charlie."

"I don't think so," Becky argued. "Her husband's a drunk. Sylvie says he spends every penny she earns on booze."

"Just talk to her, Becks!"

Maybe Audrey would blurt out some tidbit on her own. Now I was just dreaming.

I grabbed my bag and waited for the elevators. Even with several to a floor, there was a long wait. I spotted Motee Ba near the entrance and went and stood next to her. Dad was outside, peering down the drive, waiting for the valet to bring our car around.

We settled in after some healthy arguments, prodded by the

honking cars that lined up behind us. Hunger was making us cranky. Dad pulled up outside the familiar golden arches. He ordered two egg and cheese sandwiches for everyone, along with hash browns and coffee.

"I want sausage on mine," Jeet piped up.

Dad ignored him. He parked right outside the restaurant but we ate in the car.

"That should keep us till lunch," Dad said.

There was a warning note in his voice. Tony skipped out to dump all the trash and we set off.

"Where are we going?" Jeet called out.

"We are driving through the Mojave desert," Dad announced. "It's just a small drive. Then we'll hit Pappa's Indian buffet before going to the casinos."

I looked at Tony. He nodded slightly. He had promised me a gondola ride. I was going to hold him to it.

Dad merged onto Interstate 15, going South.

"We're getting close to our destination," Dad murmured to Sally.

She smiled.

I didn't think we would go all the way to California today. All our stuff was still in the hotel. Motee Ba voiced my thoughts and Dad assured her we were going back to Vegas. He smiled at Sally from the corner of his eye.

I looked out of the window. The road stretched for miles ahead and then snaked up an incline. Dad told Jeet to stay sharp.

"Welcome to California!" Jeet suddenly cried out as we crossed the state border.

A sign for the welcome center came up.

"We won't stop here today," Dad said.

We spotted the sign for the Mojave National Preserve and Dad took that exit.

"There's over a million acres of desert here," Dad preached. "And many mountain ranges. This is also one of the few places in the world where you'll find Joshua trees."

Did I mention Dad is happiest when he's in pedantic mode?

I really wanted to see the Joshua trees.

The road was deserted with not a single car in sight. Mountain ranges lined the horizon, with snow covered peaks. We came across a patch where there was a lot of snow on the ground. There were peculiar shrubs everywhere in a faded yellow color. And then we spotted the Joshua trees. Dad pulled up on the shoulder and we all got out.

A massive field of Joshua trees stretched before us, juxtaposed against a backdrop of the stark mountains. It was a beautiful sight. We took lots of pictures. Half an hour went by without any cars passing by. Someone wanted a snack so Motee Ba handed over some trail mix from the car.

"We need to leave now!" Pappa suddenly ordered, looking at his watch.

We were all quiet as Dad completed a loop and left the park to merge back onto the Interstate. We stopped at another fast food place. I ordered milk shakes and sodas. The girl who got our drinks looked me in the eye as she slapped the check down on the table.

"Teenagers!" I muttered under my breath. "Probably running late to meet a guy."

Tony hid a smile. We slurped our drinks and I picked up the piece of paper. The paper was thin and cheap and I could see something scribbled on the other side. I turned the paper over and stared with my mouth open.

I handed the paper over to Tony. Something clicked in his brain and he stared back at me.

"What did I say?" I mouthed.

A familiar smiley face with a flower stared at me from the back of the receipt. A phone number was scribbled below it.

"It's just a prank," Tony said grimly. "She must be out somewhere. Probably wants money for a smoke."

He rushed out and I waited, tapping my fingers. Tony was back in five minutes.

"I didn't see anyone."

Now he would tell me to ignore it. That is exactly what I planned to do for a change.

We reached Vegas without any more curious incidents and Dad entered the downtown area. Pappa was leaning forward in his seat, tapping his cane.

"There. There it is!"

Pappa was like a kid in a candy store. He acted like he had been kept away from Indian food for years. No one else wanted to admit how much they appreciated a home style meal after a week on the road.

"Now I need a nap," Pappa declared. "Drop us back at the hotel."

Everyone wanted a nap so we went back. The boys watched TV and discussed the different dinner buffets available.

"We are here all day tomorrow, right?" Tony asked.

I nodded. Vegas can get really tiring so Dad had planned to stay here for four whole days.

"So we're doing the gondola ride this evening, and then we'll hit the buffet."

"Gondola ride? You mean like a boat ride?" Jeet wanted to know.

"You're not coming!" I said sharply.

He looked hurt but then he grinned naughtily.

"Oh, so it's a date?"

Tony looked uncomfortable. Jeet began giving him a hard time.

The room phone rang, and I answered. It was the front desk with a message for me. Stan had requested a call back. I dialed his number, my fingers crossed behind my back.

"Meera, you said I could call the hotel," he began.

I assured him it was fine.

"Anything new?" I sucked in a breath.

"Leo's autopsy results are back. It was an overdose alright. There's a couple of curious things though."

I waited for Stan to continue.

"They found some sand on his shoes. We're not sure where it came from."

"There's no sand in Swan Creek, is there?" I knew the answer to that.

"Not naturally occurring, no."

"Did he go to a beach when he went out with his friends?"

"That's the thing," Stan said. "We could never contact his friends. So we don't really know where he went."

I was as stumped as Stan.

"You wouldn't know who his friends were?" Stan asked hopefully.

I assured him I had no idea who Leo had met in Ponca City.

"Maybe it's from a local place," Stan said. "I'll ask around."

That didn't sound too promising.

"One more thing, Meera." Stan hesitated. "The autopsy's done. Do you know if…"

My eyes filled up as I realized what Stan was asking. No one was waiting to claim Leo.

"Let me talk to a few people," I said, barely able to get the words out.

I dialed the diner and Sylvie answered. I got to the point.

"We can wait until you people get back. Talk to your grandpa, Meera."

Thinking about next of kin reminded me of Bandit.

"What happened to Charlie's dog, do you know?"

"I completely forgot!" Sylvie sounded shocked. "I'll talk to Audrey when she gets here."

Chances were he had run away in all the confusion. I sobered at the thought of him wandering around Swan Creek. I hung up and brought Tony up to speed on the calls.

He scratched his head as he processed it.

"The sand rings a bell but I don't know what. It will come to me."

"Did Leo mention going to a beach?" I quipped.

"No. I hardly talked to him. It's something else."

I went to Motee Ba's room for some much needed comfort. Pappa was asleep but she promised to talk to him later.

"It's the least we can do for him," she said quietly.

I knew she was talking about Leo.

Chapter 24

Tony held my hand as we walked out of the Bellagio. We went up the bridge that flanked the Las Vegas Strip. It would take us across to the Venetian. We searched for a good spot on the bridge to take photos. The Strip stretched in both directions, with colorful, larger than life signs of all the casinos and hotels.

"Cute couple," the girl who clicked our photo said, handing back the camera to Tony.

"We're not…" I began, but she was already out of sight in the crowd.

"You look beautiful!" Tony breathed, roving an eye over me from head to toe.

I felt beautiful. I was wearing one of the dresses we had bought in the Forum Shops and it was a sunny yellow color, perfect for Spring. The Venetian has a Grand Canal that is just like the real thing, along with bistros and cafes.

The sun was just setting and the weather was pleasant. I chose an outdoor ride and the gondolier made sure we were comfortable. We posed for pictures again and then he sang a song as we glided on the clear blue water. I imagined myself in Venice, although I was sure the water there wouldn't be this clean.

"We'll get there one day," Tony whispered in my ear.

The gondolier ducked his head as we passed under a bridge. Real or not, it was a fantastic experience. It put a smile on my face.

We strolled along the Venetian streets, staring up at the blue sky. This sky is one of my favorite features in Vegas. It changes colors, becomes cloudy and stormy. Lightning flashed and thunder boomed, and it started raining. We rushed to the nearest store. My smile widened when I noticed they sold chocolates.

We got some assorted truffles for everyone and sat down to enjoy a bowl of ice cream. Someone brushed past me and I got goose bumps as I felt a rough hand slide over me.

"Hey!" I yelled.

"What's the matter?" Tony cried, springing up from his seat.

"I just got groped."

People from adjoining tables turned around and looked at us. I was a bit shook up.

"Are you alright?" the girl from the shop wanted to know.

I gave her a brief nod. My hand was shaking. This kind of a thing had never happened to me. I dipped my head, trying to hide the tears that had welled up in my eyes. Then I saw the wad of paper in my lap.

"Tony!"

I picked up the crumpled paper and smoothed it out. The message was brief and to the point.

'Outside – Fountain - Five minutes.'

I was going to get to the bottom of this.

"Let's go, Tony."

I handed him the paper and started walking. Tony followed without a word and we almost jogged outside. There's a big fountain outside the casino and I assumed that's where we were supposed to go.

I was a bit out of breath by the time we reached the fountain. There was quite a crowd around it. People were tossing pennies in the water, making wishes and taking photos. A cool mist off the water sprayed my back and I shivered. Both Tony and I were looking around, trying to spot something unusual.

A voice spoke in my ear.

"Follow me!"

The hooded figure had moved ten feet away by the time I caught on. I hurried after it, furious at being led on some kind of chase.

Tony rushed past me and clamped his hand on the hood.

"Wait up, dude!"

The figure turned and a young girl stared back at us, frightened. Her eyes were sunken, and her cheekbones stood out against her pale face.

"Please don't hurt me," she pleaded.

"Why would I do that?" Tony asked mystified. "And what's going on?"

"I'm just the messenger," the girl said. "We're almost there."

She cut through an alley between stores and took us to some back street. An abandoned gazebo stood to a side in a small overgrown garden.

The girl made a queer bird like noise and a group of kids walked out from behind a wall.

"Are you Meera Patel?" one of the kids asked.

He was older than the girl and seemed to be the leader of the group. I tried not to stare at his clothes. They had seen better days but they were clean. A toe peeped out of his shoe.

"Who are you?" I got to the point.

"You can call me Jack," he said. "This is Jill."

He pointed to a girl standing next to him.

"What about the others?"

He nodded at the other boy and girl and they walked away and disappeared into the twilight.

"They don't need to be here."

"Are you threatening us?" Tony asked. "People know where we are. They'll call the cops if we don't get back soon."

"We don't want to harm you," Jack said, holding his arms up. "We just want to talk."

"What's with all the drama?" I asked him.

Jack pointed to a seat built into the gazebo. We climbed two steps and sat on the bench like thing. Jill and Jack sat down on the floor in front of us. There was a ratty rug on the floor next to them and it struck a chord.

"We are Leo's friends," Jack began.

"The ones he met in Ponca City?" I asked hopefully.

He shook his head.

"No. I don't know about that but if they are one of us, we can find out."

"Who are you exactly? How did you know Leo?"

Tony held up a hand.

"Before you answer that, tell me how you know Meera? And how did you know where she was?"

"Leo told us about you," Jack said. "He said you were going to take him in. Is that true?"

I nodded.

The girl's expression changed. She looked at me hungrily, as if I held the key to some treasure she wanted.

"You seem like a good person," Jack paused.

He was choosing his words carefully.

"And Leo said you are smart. So we decided to talk to you."

"Why don't you get to the point?" Tony asked impatiently.

I put my hand over Tony's, silently asking him to settle down.

"Who are you, really? Why don't you tell me the truth? Then we can talk about what I can do for you."

"We are thorks," the girl blurted out.

"I'm sorry, what now?"

"T-H-O-R-K," Jack spelled it out. "It's an acronym for Throwaway, Homeless and Runaway Kids."

"Are you part of some organization?" Tony asked.

"More like a secret group," Jack admitted. "And we are as good as invisible."

I raised my eyebrows, asking him to go on.

"We are the kids no one wants, no one cares about. We have either been abandoned by our parents or relatives, or we have chosen to run away because we couldn't bear to live on in certain conditions."

"Don't they have foster homes and stuff for kids like you?" Tony asked.

"We live under the radar. We are not in the system."

I was speechless. So was Tony.

"No one's looking for you?" Tony finally asked.

Jack shrugged.

"Where does Leo come in?" I asked.

"Leo was one of us. Then he met that old guy. The guy offered him a home and Leo went along with him."

We knew Leo was an orphan. But none of us had imagined he was literally living on the streets. Charlie Gibson had done a good deed.

"Leo lived in Oklahoma. You live here in Nevada."

"He was part of our study group," Jill said. "He was one of the smarter ones. He always got good grades."

"You go to school?" I asked, astounded.

I wondered if these kids even got two square meals a day. And they were talking about study groups.

"We home-school," Jack smirked, giving me a knowing look.

"We are good kids, Meera. We've just had a raw deal in life."

I gulped, not knowing what to say.

"The THORK are the good guys," Jill said. "We don't do drugs or cheat or steal. We work on getting our GED so we can go to college or get a job. We just have to stay afloat until we turn 18."

"No one can force us then," Jack said seriously.

"Did you write letters?" I asked. "How did you study together?"

Jack and Jill looked at me like I was an extra terrestrial.

"Aren't you an engineer, Meera? We communicate via email."

I felt suitably chastened.

"There's an online group we created. We use it like a message board. It comes in handy. We use email for any personal communication."

Where did these kids get access to email?

"Public libraries," Jill said. "As long as we don't stick to a place too long, we are fine."

"There's an art to it," Jack said proudly. "It keeps us on our toes."

"How did you know where to find me?"

"Leo said you were on this road trip. You were spotted in different places. We got updates from our people."

"And those smiley faces? Were they for me?"

Jack smiled.

"Just a couple of them, the ones you saw in Vegas. They are part of our code."

"What kind of code?" I asked, fascinated.

"We have a system," Jill said. "It's like a secret language. We leave clues behind us for other THORKs."

"But why?"

"So we have each other's back," Jack said grimly. "There aren't many people looking out for us, you know."

I thought of the symbols I had seen in Texas and New Mexico.

"We are all over," Jack nodded.

"I saw the symbols in rest areas, on barns, even on cars."

"They mean different things. Some are just motivational, like the flower with the smile. It means keep going, everything will be fine. Then there's an inverted triangle that stands for drugs. It's a warning to get out of the area. There's signs for food, and for barters. See, some people don't care we are homeless. A kind lady might offer a meal, or a ride on the highway. Some places let us wash dishes in exchange for a bed at night. Some doctors treat us for free when we are sick. Some teachers help us with our lessons."

"And you have symbols for all of this?"

My mouth was hanging open.

Jill nodded.

"There's still a lot of kind people in this world."

"How often does someone find a home? You know, like Leo did?"

"Doesn't happen often," Jack admitted. "Leo was one of the lucky ones. Or so we thought."

We all knew how that had turned out.

"All this is hard to take in," I said.

"You better believe it," Jack said. "We have broken every rule to get in touch with you."

I sensed what was coming. Jill spelled it out for me.

"We want you to find out who killed Leo."

Chapter 25

I stared back at Jack and Jill.

"You think I haven't tried? I'm up against a wall. The police are convinced he took his life."

"That's impossible. We can vouch for it."

"Really?" I pursed my mouth. "You don't exist as far as the world is concerned. Who's going to take you at your word?"

"They don't have to. Leo was looking forward to his new life. He said it himself in the messages he posted. That has to count for something, right?"

I thought back to when I last spoke to Leo. It was sometime in the morning. Had he been in touch with anyone since then?

"He posted a message on the boards soon as he came home from jail. He told us you and that other lady had offered him a home. He was happy. He turns 18 in the fall, you see. And he was very close to finishing his school work."

"We were ready to put him up for as long as he wanted."

Jack nodded. "He could work once he turned 18."

"I have a gas station," Tony said. "I could have let him have a few hours. But he never said anything."

"Your town is pretty small," Jack said. "It's best to lie low in such places. He didn't mingle with a lot of people. And he couldn't apply for small jobs since that required paperwork."

"Did Charlie know all this?" I asked.

"Sure did. He said he was a lonely guy who didn't socialize much. Leo just had to follow some house rules and keep up with his school work."

Charlie Gibson was set in his ways. So no one expected him to change his ways overnight just because a teenager was living with him. People had wondered how Leo had fallen in line with Charlie's austere lifestyle. Now we knew. A kid in his position would have done anything to have a safe place to live in.

I tried to bring the conversation back on track.

"So he said someone was taking him in," I repeated. "Was that the last time you spoke to him?"

I noticed Jack's face assume an eager expression by the time I finished my sentence.

"No, it wasn't. We were chatting on Instant Messenger. He was getting his stuff, putting together a bag to take to this diner lady."

"Right."

"He found something," Jack said. "He wouldn't say what. But he was finding it hard to keep it a secret."

"What did he find?" Tony asked, finally taking an interest in the conversation.

"He said he needed to go talk to someone."

"What time was this?" I asked.

"Around three his time," Jack said. "He was going to come back online to tell me how it went. He told me to keep my fingers crossed."

"Did you talk to him again?"

Jack's expression told me the story.

"I logged in a couple of times in the evening, but there wasn't anything from him. We didn't hear from him again until we read the story in the newspaper."

"You didn't try and call him?" I blurted out.

"We don't have that kind of money," Jack said grimly.

"I understand how you feel," I said. "But like I said, no one's listening to me on this one."

"We want justice for Leo. Once word gets around that he was a homeless kid, no one will ever help us. We will lose the faint ray of hope we have, that 1% chance that one of us will find a home."

Jill spoke up.

"He was our friend. Someone thought they could kill him in cold blood just because he had no support system."

"That too," Jack said sheepishly. "We'll help you in any way possible. We can't pay you much, but we can work something out."

"I don't want your money," I protested. "I'm not a professional or anything."

"We don't care about that, as long as you get results."

I leaned back and closed my eyes.

"So these friends Leo was meeting in Ponca City? Did he actually know them, or was it some kind of meeting for your group?"

"We don't have meetings," Jill said. "Kids run into each other in different places. Most of us are pretty cool. We share whatever we have. Meals, blankets, clothes – you run into someone a couple of times, you become friends."

"Leo said these people were on Spring Break, driving to the coast and to Florida."

"They must have been ex-THORKS," Jack said promptly. "Kids over 18, you know. Some of them keep in touch."

"Can you find out who they were?"

"We can put a word out," Jack said. "Why?"

"The cops found some sand on Leo's shoes. Chances are he went to the beach with these kids. I just want to check if he really did."

"We can find that out for you," Jack promised.

"I might be able to talk to some people once I get home," I said. "But I can't do much from here."

Jack's face turned hopeful.

"So you'll work on this for us?"

"Leo seemed like a good kid. If anyone harmed him on purpose, I'll do my best to find out who did it."

Jack held out his hand and I shook it. I gave Tony a meaningful look. He stared back at me, uncomprehending. Tony can be so dumb sometimes.

"How about a burger on us?" I asked Jack.

He looked hurt.

"We don't want anything from you."

Tony had finally caught on and was holding out a 20. Both the kids stared at the note longingly. But they didn't budge.

"Please, from one friend to another."

Jack looked very young all of a sudden. He hesitated, then took the money.

"You're too kind, Meera."

We said goodbye and Tony and I stood up to leave. Neither of us talked about when we would meet again. If they had something for me, they would find me.

We cut across the dark alley we had come through and hit the Strip again. It was lit up like ten Christmases. I sighed with relief.

"Did you notice that blanket?" Tony whispered.

"They must be sleeping in that gazebo," I murmured.

"For how long, Meera?"

"Until someone turns them out, I guess."

We waded through the crowds that thronged the sidewalk and climbed over the bridge. At times like these, I wonder what I have done to deserve my life of luxury. Money flowed around me like water. The over the top lights and neon signs, the casinos where people gambled away money, the shops where they spent a pretty penny were all examples of the infamous Vegas debauchery. How many of the people milling around would spare five bucks for a hungry kid?

Tony sensed my mood and stayed quiet. We were taking a cab to one end of the Strip, hitting a dinner buffet Jeet had picked out. The family was gathered around inside the Bellagio lobby, waiting for us.

I hugged Motee Ba and kissed her on the cheek. We split into two cabs and headed to dinner.

The dinner buffet was bigger and better than the breakfast. They even had a section for Indian food which made Pappa happy. Sweet and spicy aromas assailed my senses and I found my appetite making a comeback. Tony and I chose to walk back to the hotel. We really needed to stretch our legs after that meal.

"You think those kids were leading us on?" Tony asked me.

"You saw them yourself. Did they look like pranksters?"

"I know you feel strongly about this," he said. "Leo's innocence, I mean."

"Unless someone comes forward with new information, there's not much I can do."

"Do you want to fly home with the others?" Tony offered. "I can get back on my own."

The rest of the family was going to fly back home from California. Tony and I were going to drive back home in the LX. We had looked forward to doing it. Driving back would add a few more days to the trip. I had taken extra time off from work for that.

"It's a bit too much for one person," I said. "What do two more days matter?"

Nothing was going to bring Leo back. But the trail was getting cold. My chances of finding any relevant information diminished as time went by.

"This is why we should have brought a rental."

"One way rentals are too expensive, Meera. And no way we could have been so comfortable in a rented car."

Tony wanted to play some slots after we got back. He still had 10 bucks left to lose out of his budget. I rolled my eyes and promised to be back soon.

It was still early and I was hoping to catch Becky at the diner. She listened spell bound as I told her about THORK.

"My God, Meera. Where do you find these people?"

"In this case, they found me!"

"I took some brownies over to Joyce Baker. Did you know she's taking care of Bandit?"

"I did wonder what happened to him."

"She found him sitting on her porch one day. He stays in her yard all day and she takes him in at night. Says she's too old to really care for him."

"Did you ask her anything?"

"I didn't have a script or anything," Becky apologized. "She seemed lonely when I met her so I thought I would pay her a visit."

"You must have talked about something."

"I think she spends a lot of time behind that curtain. She reports on everything that goes on in that street. She saw Leo head out in Charlie's car that afternoon. Then she saw him come back later that night."

"She did? She must be the last person to see Leo alive. Did she say what time that was?"

"9:30 PM. Said he was already getting out of hand, staying out past his curfew. Charlie never let him go out after dinner."

"Does she know Leo's dead?"

"She has to. She knows everything else."

"What else did you do today?"

"Just my usual work day," Becky sighed. "It's a bit of a drag without you."

"I know. I miss you too. There's so much to tell you."

"Oh, I forgot. Audrey came in for lunch. And I think I know who's funding her latest lifestyle."

"Don't make me guess, Becks!"

"Charlie Gibson."

"What?"

"She'd been asking for a raise for some time. Her work doubled since Leo came in to live with Charlie. But Leo helped her with the laundry and stuff. So Charlie didn't think she deserved a raise. They had been at it for a while. Then Charlie gave her a bonus all of a sudden."

"And she's spending it all?"

"She's given a good amount of it to Sylvie, it seems. Wants to be able to come in to the diner and relax. Doesn't want her husband spending it all on booze, she said."

"Smart girl!" I said approvingly.

"She said it was time for her to take care of herself."

"What made Charlie give her the money all of a sudden?"

"He'd been in a good mood since the weekend. She has no idea why. He wrote out her check before heading to Sylvie's to enjoy the meatloaf. He told her she better treat Leo right. He was going to be a big guy one day."

"Now why would he say that?"

"Maybe Leo aced an exam or something."

"Must have been something else, Becks. Charlie always knew Leo was good at school work."

"She said Leo was a good kid. He gave her a ride somewhere when he didn't have to."

"When was that?" I asked sharply.

"Must've been the day he…"

"Can you confirm it, please? And ask Joyce about it too. Ask if Audrey was in the car when she saw Leo head out that afternoon."

"What if she was?"

"We might be able to guess where Leo was headed."

We wrapped up our call and I hung up. I went over the entire conversation in my mind, and noted down a few points. I wanted to follow up on them with Stan. I felt I had missed something but I couldn't put my finger on it. I just hoped it would come back to me later.

Chapter 26

We gathered around in Motee Ba's room again the next morning. Jeet and Tony had gone down to the café and brought coffee and an assortment of pastries for everyone. No one wanted a big breakfast after last night's dinner.

"I can't wait to get home and make some *khichdi*," Motee Ba sighed.

Khichdi is a rice and lentil dish that's a Gujarati staple. Served with ghee and a buttermilk stew, it's our comfort food.

Everyone wanted to do something different that day. I sipped my coffee, listening to them argue about it.

"Why don't we split up?" Tony asked. "We can all do whatever we want. It's our last day in Vegas."

"On one condition," Dad said. "We're having dinner together."

Sally smiled at him and nodded.

Motee Ba wanted to do some shopping, Pappa wanted to rest in his room, the boys each wanted to check out a different casino. I wanted some quiet time to think about what might have happened to Leo.

I settled down in the overstuffed chair in my room, and looked down on the Strip. People moved about like ants, lining sidewalks, dodging yellow cabs, laughing and enjoying themselves. The front desk called with another message. I had missed Stan's call again.

I wondered if I should tell Stan Miller about THORK. There was no saying how he would act on it. He might feel compelled to report them. He was a cop after all. I decided to keep the THORK out of the conversation.

I dialed Stan's number. The calling card warned me I only had one minute worth of talk time left.

"Can you call me back?" I pleaded. "I'm plumb out of minutes."

I hung up and the phone rang almost immediately.

"How's it going, Stan?" I asked.

"I keep thinking about the sand we found on Leo's shoes," he said. "There is only one place in Swan Creek that has sand."

"Don't hold back," I drawled.

"The Palms, Meera! You remember how they brought in all that white sand from some place in Texas, just so those nabobs had a sandy beach around that lake of theirs?"

The Palms at Swan Creek is a super luxurious housing compound on the South edge of town. Simply referred to as 'The Palms', it houses some of the richest people in the county. Some of these just inherited the wealth, some earned it, and some married into it. They have their own posh club inside their compound, an eighteen hole golf course and a big manmade lake, large enough for all kinds of water sports. The place is an urban legend because most people in town have never actually been inside that compound. That includes me, of course.

The smallest lot size in The Palms is ten acres, with most estates being thirty plus acres, with their own woods and ponds.

"You think Leo Smith went to The Palms?"

I couldn't hold back my laughter.

"It's an option, Meera."

Stan sounded a bit hurt. I have often criticized him for not thinking outside the box. Here he was, considering various scenarios, and I had laughed at him.

"I may be able to get some information about where Leo went with his friends."

Stan wanted to know more but I told him to wait until I had something solid.

"What time did Leo take those pills?"

"Time of death is between 4 – 8 PM, Meera."

Something clicked in my mind, and I realized what had bothered me since last night. My heart beat faster as I realized the implications.

"Are you sure about this, Stan?" I asked urgently. "Could there be any leeway in that?"

"I can ask, but they take that into account in a range as wide as that."

"Joyce Baker saw Leo drive back at 9:30 PM."

Stan let out a curse.

"That's impossible," he said flatly.

"She saw Leo drive out in Charlie's car around 4 PM and come back in the same car at 9:30. She mentioned how he was breaking his curfew."

"Why didn't she say something?"

"Did you talk to her after Leo died?"

Stan's silence was answer enough.

"Leo left a suicide note."

The police had accepted Leo took his own life. So there hadn't been any investigation. I remembered what Becky had told me about Audrey Jones.

"He dropped Audrey off somewhere. Maybe he told her where he was headed?"

"I'm going to talk to these two women," Stan promised. "Now."

I felt a tiny sliver of anticipation. I told Stan to call me as soon as he learned something more.

I paced the room, feeling stifled. I picked up my bag and rushed out, eager for some fresh air. It took me twenty minutes to actually step out of the hotel. I started walking along the Strip, lost in thought. If Leo had died before 8 PM, when had he come back to Charlie's? Had someone taken Charlie's car out again?

Had Joyce really seen the car? She might have confused it with some other day. That seemed like the simplest explanation.

Then I began to think of who might have had access to Charlie's house or his car. Don Collins came to mind. But what did he have against Leo? Had Leo known something incriminating about Don? Maybe he saw Don and Charlie have a fight. Or he heard Don threaten Charlie. Don might have wanted to get Leo out of the way. But why did he need Charlie's car, especially on that night?

I walked for what seemed like hours but was actually maybe forty minutes. I began to feel hungry. I looked around and realized I had almost reached downtown. Souvenir shops clustered around one corner and a pizza shop lay next to it. I could smell the sauce and the mozzarella as I walked toward it. A curious bird like sound rent the air. I looked around. Jack was peeping out from behind a corner.

I nodded at him, calling him over. He looked around before coming out in the open.

"Hi Meera!" he said.

"How about some lunch?" I asked.

"I don't want to impose," he began.

"I'm starving, Jack. Help me out here, will you?"

He put his hands in the kangaroo pocket of his hoodie and followed me, head down.

"Is Jill around here somewhere?" I asked. "Go get her, will you?"

He gave the slightest nod to someone outside the window. Jill walked in shyly. I hadn't even noticed she was standing outside the shop.

I put in an order for a large pizza and got drinks and garlic bread for us.

"I hope you like sausage," I said, placing the bread down on the table.

"We have some news," Jack began.

"Let's eat first," I said, picking up a hunk of the cheesy garlic bread.

They hesitated, then followed.

A server brought a huge pizza and placed it on the table, along with plates and napkins. Steam rose off the pizza, and the scent of spicy Italian sausage and rich tomato sauce made my mouth water. There was a healthy layer of melted mozzarella on top, oozing off the edges.

"Do you like it?" I asked Jack and Jill. "Or do you want something else?"

They ate tentatively and I marveled at their self control. Jill stopped after the first slice. I had an aha moment.

"I hear they have great meatball subs. Why don't we get some to go?"

I went to the counter and put in an order for the subs. The kids finally relaxed and helped me polish off the pizza.

"You're spoiling us, Meera," Jack grinned.

I feigned surprise and told them to save room for dessert.

"We heard back from the guys Leo met," Jack began after he had carefully wiped his mouth.

"Any luck?"

"They did go to the beach, but not with Leo."

"They wanted Leo to go with them," Jill added. "But he wanted to get back home to Charlie. He just spent the night with them."

"What do these kids do?" I asked.

"They work," Jack said. "They'll be going to college next year."

"Would they be willing to talk to a friend of mine?"

"You mean the police, don't you?" Jack quailed.

"It may not be necessary," I hastened to assure him. "Forget it."

Jack wrote something down on a piece of paper and handed it over.

"This is my email id. You can send me an email anytime."

It was like déjà vu. I remembered how I had given Leo my email id at Charlie's memorial service.

"I gave Leo my email," I murmured. "But I don't think I have his."

"It's justleosmith at yahoo," Jill rattled off. "Guess he won't be using it anymore."

We sobered, thinking of Leo.

I wrote my own email on another paper napkin and handed it to Jack.

"Here's my email. Feel free to get in touch. And if you ever travel through Oklahoma, you're welcome to pay us a visit."

Both Jack and Jill grew emotional, but tried to hide it. I felt sad when I realized they didn't have anyone to turn to in a crisis. No shoulder to cry on. No safety net.

"I mean it, kids. You can ask me about college too when the time comes. I know a trick or two about those college applications."

"Leo said you dropped out of college," Jack smirked.

"Where did he hear that?" I acted surprised. "And it was graduate school."

"You're alright, Meera," Jack smiled.

"Did Leo ever tell you how he met Charlie? Or where?"

"It's the stuff of dreams," Jill said. "We were all on our way to New Orleans. Leo got a job helping some people move in. He said he would catch up with us later. He caught a ride with Charlie. They got talking. Charlie offered to take him home. Just like that."

"And Leo trusted him?" I asked.

"He did. Leo said he sensed Charlie would treat him well."

Charlie Gibson may not have hugged Leo every morning, but he had done well by him. No one could have predicted the sticky end they would both come to.

"I'm going to do my best to find Leo's killer," I told Jack. "That's a promise."

We stepped out of the restaurant and I handed over the sandwich bag.

"Stay safe, you two."

Jill hugged me impulsively and I hugged her back, trying to hold back my tears.

"What are you waiting for?" I asked Jack, folding him into the hug.

Jill handed me a paper. It had a whole bunch of the doodles along with a legend next to them.

"Just in case you want to support a THORK," she said softly.

I couldn't wait to show them to Motee Ba and Sylvie. I was sure we would be painting some of these on the side of the diner, and on our garage doors.

I said one final goodbye and started walking back to the hotel. I wanted to do something to help the THORKs.

A thought was already forming in my mind.

Chapter 27

I collapsed on my bed back at the hotel, panting from the exertion. The hotel desk had another message from Stan. I was glad I had stopped on the way to get a new calling card.

"Hey Stan!" I said, still breathing somewhat heavily. "What's up?"

"Wait till you hear this, Meera."

I fluffed the pillows and settled back against the headboard. Stan sounded like he had found something new.

"That Joyce Baker is something else. She had no idea Leo was dead!"

"What?"

"We asked her if she was sure she saw Leo. She told us how Charlie had a strict curfew for the boy. He was not supposed to go out after dinner."

"But dinner at Charlie's was at 6:30 every day."

"That's right. The only place that kid was allowed to go to was the library. And that was between breakfast and lunch."

I sort of knew why Charlie might have imposed these rules. But I wasn't going to share.

"And she saw Leo drive back that night?"

"She was sure at first. But then we told her Leo had been found dead. That was a big shock for her."

"Isn't she the busybody? How did she miss the cops coming in to take Leo away?"

"She had a doctor's appointment that morning. So she never saw that. She'd been wondering why she hasn't seen Leo around."

"What about the car?" I asked.

"She wasn't so sure once she learnt about Leo. She saw the car come in, but she didn't see who was driving. She just assumed it was Leo."

"What does that mean for us?" I cried.

"That's not all, Meera. She thinks Don Collins may have something to do with it."

"What? Becky says she's afraid of Anna and her son. She begins to shake every time Becky mentions them."

"That's obvious," Stan said. "She pointed the finger at Don the moment we told her about Leo. Said he had it in for Charlie."

"Charlie? But what about Leo?"

"Joyce Baker says she saw Don come out of Charlie's window the night Charlie was killed. So she figures Don stabbed him."

"Why didn't she say anything all this time?" I could guess the answer to that.

"Anna threatened her. Told her she'd best keep her mouth shut about what she sees on the street."

"Does this mean Don killed Charlie?"

"We don't know. We are bringing him in now. He's a hardened criminal, Meera. I don't think he'll own up to it that easily."

"What do you think happened to Leo then?"

"We are beginning to think there might be something fishy."

I pumped my fist in the air. Would the police finally start treating Leo's death as a murder?

"Did you talk to Audrey?" I pressed on.

"I did," Stan said. "Leo dropped her off near the city offices. She had some bills to pay. He said he had to go farther out."

The city offices were in the center of town. Leo could have gone anywhere after that.

"Could someone else have seen him that day?"

"We are asking around, Meera."

"Did Joyce say anything else? Maybe someone visited Leo at the house? Doesn't she notice these things?"

"We didn't ask her about visitors. But that's a good question."

Stan hung up and I closed my eyes, trying to settle the turmoil in my mind. Thoughts were flying around and I couldn't help but wonder if I had missed something. Did Don Collins have a strong enough motive to kill Charlie? What about Leo? What could Don have against him?

I shuffled through my index cards and put a line through the stuff we had ruled out in the last couple of days. I started a new card for Jack and wrote down what he had said. Leo had been excited about something. Then I remembered what Audrey had said about Charlie's mood.

What had made both Charlie and Leo perk up all of a sudden?

I heard some commotion outside and the boys burst in, looking excited.

"Get ready, Meera!" Jeet cried. "We're going on a ride."

"Nothing too scary," Tony added.

He knows I'm not big on rides.

"It's a 3D ride, starting in 30 minutes. We need to get going now."

Jeet was ready to combust.

"It's next door at Caesar's," Tony added. "But it will take us that long to walk there and get the tickets."

I went along with them, glad for the diversion. The ride turned out to be something to do with Atlantis, that mythical city. We strapped ourselves into the seats and got rattled around as we rode through some kind of obstacle course. I didn't care for it and I almost threw up.

"You're looking horrible," Jeet laughed as we came out.

I preferred not to voice my thoughts.

"I need a nap. Do you know where we are going tonight?"

"Uncle Andy's booked a table for all of us. It's a surprise."

I grabbed a coffee from the café in the hotel and threw in a chocolate cupcake. Maybe my head would stop pounding after I ate something. The hot coffee and the chocolate soothed me and I dozed off, watching an old sitcom on TV. The phone woke me up. It was Stan again.

"Third time's the charm, hunh?" I joked.

"Don Collins started talking."

I sat up. Was it going to be that easy?

"He admits to going into Charlie's house that night," Stan started. "He was a bit drunk, I think, although he won't admit it. He said he had a few beers. He had been spoiling for a fight. He said Charlie had no business turning him in."

"What was he going to do? Slap Charlie around?"

"There's no way to know that. Both Leo and Charlie are always in after 6:30. But Leo left that day and he took Charlie's car. Don had a few more drinks, trying to drum up the courage to go confront Charlie."

"And?"

"He finally went and knocked on the door. He said it was open. He walked in and saw Charlie lying there in that hallway. He was already dead."

"Why didn't he call the cops?"

"Because, Meera. He had just got out of jail. He had no good reason for being there. But he did take some money out of Charlie's wallet."

"Once a thief…"

"Something like that. Then he must have lost his mind because he jumped out of the window instead of going back out of that door."

"I'm surprised he didn't run away."

"He thought that would have been more suspicious. So he decided to sit tight. He talked to his mother and they thought Joyce might have seen him jump from the window. She's always right there, hiding behind her curtains."

"So Anna made up a story."

"Yeah. She thought she would come forward and say she saw an intruder, and then be her son's alibi."

"Why did she point a finger at Leo?"

"When they heard the police were questioning Leo, she thought she'd improve on her story. They thought Leo had even less credibility than her son, being an orphan and all."

I was stunned. The plan sounded foolproof. Anna had thought of a lot of angles. Leo would have found it hard to disprove this theory.

"They wouldn't have succeeded, Meera. Especially after you got here and talked to people."

"What did they miss?"

"We talked to Audrey too. Guess who gave her a ride the night Charlie died?"

"Leo?" I asked, amazed.

"Righto! He offered her a ride home, since he was taking the car out anyway. She waited until he wrapped up his sandwich and they left together."

"How can you be sure Don's telling the truth?"

"We talked to Joyce again. She saw Don go in and saw him jump out of that window. The question is, what did he do while he was inside that house?"

"I assume the knife didn't have his fingerprints?"

Stan answered in the negative.

"But he did intend to harm Charlie?"

"He wanted to teach him a lesson. We can only guess what he might have done."

I thought a bit.

"Charlie and Don had a history, right?"

"I'd say that!"

"Charlie wouldn't have turned his back on Don."

"That's a good point, Meera."

"Does this mean you have cleared Leo of any involvement in Charlie's death?"

"It does look like he was innocent."

"You need to say that for the record, Stan. He deserves that."

"We can discuss it when you get back, Meera. Aren't you ready to come home?"

I sighed. I may have physically traveled across a bunch of states, but my heart and head had both stayed in Swan Creek.

"Did you confirm the time of Leo's death?" I asked Stan.

He had. Leo had most probably lost his life around 5 PM.

"We have a theory," Stan began. "It's only a theory at this point," he warned. "Leo may have been killed somewhere else."

"You think someone brought him back and staged the whole thing?"

Stan refused to say any more.

"I still think the sand we found on Leo's shoes is important. And the only place around here that has anything like it is the Palms."

"You can't go knocking on doors over there? Ask people if they saw Leo?"

"We might, only if we knew Leo had a reason to go there. He wouldn't have got past the gates unless someone cleared him from inside."

"Maybe you can talk to the guards at the Palms?" I suggested.

"Those folks are pretty tight lipped. Think they are a notch above the police. Better paid, too."

"Dial back a second, Stan. You are ready to believe Leo didn't kill himself?"

Stan was noncommittal.

"I guess so."

"Do you have any idea of the grief I have got over this? My Dad has said all kinds of nasty things about Leo. Wait till I tell him I was right."

"Don't be hasty, Meera."

"I've always believed Leo was innocent. After all this new evidence, I'm convinced he was victimized. There's no way I'm letting this rest now, Stan."

Stan grunted but said nothing.

"You better be prepared, Stan. Once I get home, I'm going to find out who killed Charlie Gibson. And who killed poor Leo. And I'm going to make sure the world knows what a good kid he was."

"Calm down, Meera. I'm with you on this one."

Stan Miller can be a bit slow on the uptake. But once he grasps something, he follows it through. I couldn't ask for a better ally.

"Thank you Stan! I'm going to hold you to it. And now, I have to go talk to my family."

Chapter 28

I flew out of my room and knocked on Motee Ba's door. I rushed in, holding Motee Ba by the shoulders. I twirled her around in circles, unable to control my excitement.

"Stop it, girl!" Pappa hollered, tapping his cane. "What have you done now?"

"Wait till you hear this," I said, including Pappa in the conversation. "Actually, I want Dad to be here when I say it."

I picked up the room phone and asked Dad to come to Motee Ba's room right away. Dad appeared two minutes later, looking tense.

"What's the matter? Is Pappa alright?"

"Everyone's fine!" Motee Ba assured him.

Dad's mouth twisted in a grimace as he looked at me.

"What's this about, Meera?"

"I just heard from Stan Miller."

Dad's face began turning a nice shade of red.

"Didn't we agree you were not going to call back home?"

"He called me," I said mildly, giving him a version of the truth. "Leo did not harm Charlie Gibson. The police have definite proof of it. And Leo did not commit suicide either. He was murdered."

There was a deathly silence in the room. No one said anything for a few seconds. Then Motee Ba spoke up.

"That poor boy!"

Dad was struggling with his emotions.

"You went behind my back, didn't you?"

"You're missing the point, Dad. You thought Leo was trash. You couldn't care less how he died because you probably thought he didn't deserve better. But he was just a poor innocent kid who got a raw deal in life."

Dad was speechless for a change.

"I'm going to get justice for Leo. When we get back, I'm going to do everything possible to get to the bottom of this."

"Bravo!" Pappa said suddenly. "I don't expect anything less from you."

"But…" Dad faltered.

"I won't say anything more on the topic, Dad, don't worry. I won't spoil your precious trip. You and Sally can hold hands and sing all you want."

I hadn't meant to say the last bit. But I often lose control once I start talking. I swept out of the room, and almost bumped into Sally. She was standing in the lobby, looking stricken.

I felt a twinge of discomfort at having taken a potshot at her.

Then I was in my room, behind the door I slammed with all my might. Things would move ahead now, I felt. I turned on all the taps and began filling the bath tub. A good long soak with lots of bubbles sounded good to me.

I dressed for dinner, wearing one of my new dresses. There was a knock on the door and Sally came in. She held up a small box for me. I stared at the dangle earrings, with tiny diamonds and a single pearl. She motioned me to try them on. They went very well with the short black dress I was wearing. Paired with silver sandals and a small silver clutch, they completed my ensemble.

Sally smiled and sat down on the bed.

"Are these for me?" I asked.

She nodded.

"Your Dad and I got them for you."

I felt myself choke up. I barely said thank you, and then it was time to go. The boys had come in and dressed while I was enjoying my bath. We were having dinner in one of the fancier restaurants in the casino.

Dad looked smart in a jacket and tie. Sally looked attractive in a red dress. I decided to ignore Dad and not mention Leo, in the interest of keeping the peace. He must have decided something similar.

Everyone made small talk, as if by some silent agreement. The food was excellent, and it wasn't too hard to concentrate on it. We savored the meal and sat back, enjoying coffee after our rich dessert.

"How's Reema doing? Have you talked to her at all?" Motee Ba asked Tony.

"She knows I'm with you, Granny," Tony grinned boyishly. "You'll keep me out of trouble."

"That's fine, dear. But maybe you should talk to her once. She must be missing you."

"I'll send her an email," Tony said airily.

The blood rushed in my ears and I stared at Tony. I had completely forgotten something all this time. He raised his eyebrows in a silent question. I shook my head and he took the hint.

Dad and Sally wanted to go for a walk. I heard Dad talking about a gondola ride. Motee Ba and Pappa were going to their room. The plan was to start early tomorrow, as soon as we finished breakfast.

I whisked Tony aside and told him about my epiphany. When you over think something, you often ignore the simplest solution. I had completely forgotten about giving Leo my email. I had even talked to Jack about it, but I never considered Leo might have written to me.

"What if…" I stared at Tony, wide eyed.

"Let's check your email, sweetie."

"But how? All the public libraries must be closed by now."

"I have a better solution," Tony smiled.

He took my hand and strode across the casino floor. I tried to keep up as we rushed through groups of people clustered around roulette wheels and blackjack tables. I had worked up a sweat by the time Tony halted in front of a large wooden door with a gold plaque labeling it as the Business Center.

"Madame!" he said with a flourish, holding the door open for me.

I feasted my eyes on a bank of the latest computers, separated by privacy screens. A large copier and laser printer were placed at one end. I even saw a scanner next to them.

"Welcome to the Bellagio!" I whistled.

I wasted no time in loading up my email.

"Better write to Aunt Reema while you're here," I reminded Tony.

I realized he was already typing a note to his Mom.

"Way ahead of ya," he smirked.

There were over a hundred new emails in my Inbox and they took some time to load. The hotel's network wasn't as fast as the one at Pioneer Poly, but it was faster than a dial up.

I stared wide eyed at the screen, scrolling through the page. I almost pinched myself when I saw one from Leo Smith.

I grabbed Tony's shoulder and pointed at the screen, dumbstruck.

"Aren't you going to open it?"

Tony placed his hand over mine and moved the mouse to click on the email. There it was, probably the last words Leo had penned to anyone.

I skimmed through the email, shocked at the contents. They were beyond my wildest imagination. Leo sounded jubilant, just like Jack had said. There was some preliminary stuff about how he was thankful he could write to me etc. Then he mentioned a possible windfall.

'If this is true, Meera, life as I know it will never be the same. But I want to confirm something before I say anything more.'

Had Leo won the lottery? I didn't know if an underage kid could play it. I decided to ask Pappa if Charlie Gibson was in the habit of buying lottery tickets.

Leo said he was heading out of the house. He needed to call on someone before he went over to Sylvie's. There was a postscript. He wanted me to check someone out if possible.

'Didn't you say you were driving all the way to the coast, Meera? I checked the map and I think this place is on your route. Would you mind checking this guy out?'

There was a post postscript.

'If this guy is legit, you'll know the whole story.'

There were a bunch of smileys after that.

I scrolled further down the page and saw an attachment. I had almost missed it. I clicked on the file and it turned out to be a visiting card. It belonged to some lawyer and the address was listed as Barstow in California.

"Is that…"

I turned around, wondering if Tony had kept up with me as I read through the email.

"That's on our way, Meera."

It wouldn't have mattered even if it wasn't.

"That's it. We have to go meet this guy tomorrow."

"Maybe we should call first?" Tony pointed to a bunch of numbers on the calling card.

"Let's print this out," I said, suddenly noticing the printer in the corner.

I printed out the email and the attachment, and looked at Tony.

"The mystery deepens," he said, and smiled.

"What is all this about, Tony?" I cried. "Why was Leo being so vague? He could have given us a hint."

"He didn't know those were going to be his last words."

I sobered at the thought. I felt angry and sad at the same time, and helpless. Could I have done something to keep Leo safe?

"It's too late to call now," Tony said, reading my mind. "We'll tackle this tomorrow."

"You think Dad will let us stop there?"

"We'll try our best to convince him. Otherwise, we'll drop them off at Sally's and turn around. Okay?"

I let Tony hug me and cried a bit.

"I'm so glad you're here."

"I know!" he smirked and ushered me out.

Jeet was watching a movie back in the room. He looked at my blotched face and rolled his eyes.

"More drama?" he said. "You better watch out, Meera. One day, you'll try his patience."

I threw a pillow at Jeet and went into the bathroom to change. Another road had opened up, and I felt hopeful. Charlie and Leo were both such loners, we had struggled over the motive for their murder. Was it all about money after all?

"Give me that remote," I ordered, coming out of the bathroom. "It's my turn to choose a movie."

"No chick flicks!" Jeet warned.

I ignored him and flipped the channels. We finally settled on a movie we all liked, and I forgot everything for a while. Jeet wanted to call room service to celebrate our last night in Vegas. The boys ordered burgers and fries and I went for a plate of pasta. We shared another ice cream sundae, and finally dozed off, our bellies full of food.

Chapter 29

We were all ready by eight the next morning. Everyone was excited about the next part of the trip, the last leg. I think we were all secretly longing to get home. We had a quick breakfast at the café downstairs and went up to get our luggage. All our bags had already been lined up near the door, ready for the bell boys to take down.

I stood by the windows one last time staring down at the Strip. Las Vegas had surprised me in more ways than one. The hotel staff arrived with a large trolley and loaded up our bags. After that, it was time to leave. We stood in the lobby, waiting for the valet to bring the car around.

Dad pulled me aside. I braced myself for a lecture.

"Meera, I am sorry about your friend. I was wrong to say all those things. Hope you won't think too badly about your old man."

I wasn't ready to forgive him that easily.

"It's okay, Dad."

"I'm with you on this, Meera. I'm willing to help any way I can."

My face split in a smile.

"In that case…"

I told him we would be making a pit stop on the way to Sally's. Dad had no choice but to agree after that statement of his.

We have never talked about where Sally actually lives. All I knew was she lived somewhere near Los Angeles. Would she able to accommodate all of us? Or were we booking into a hotel? The time to learn that had come. I guess we would know in a few hours.

Tony had called the number on the business card from Leo's email and made an appointment for us. We would reach Barstow by 11 if we didn't hit too much traffic.

Tony merged onto I-15 South, the same road we had taken on our trip to the Mojave Desert.

"We have had a wonderful time, haven't we?" Motee Ba said.

"Yes, Hansa. But I am ready to go home now."

Pappa must be so tired. It was amazing how he had endured so much time on the road.

Barstow was a natural stop on the road between Vegas and LA. So we weren't really going out of the way. Tony dropped everyone off outside a sandwich shop.

"Meera and I have to go somewhere. Will you be alright here until then?"

Dad gave a brief nod. Pappa didn't look too happy at being dumped in the middle of nowhere.

"Don't take too long," he warned.

Tony pulled up outside a small building a couple of blocks away. The sign pronounced it as the office of Robert Eckerman & Associates. We pushed the door open and entered a small reception area. A private office lay beyond it.

"Come on in," a voice called out.

An older man stood up from a plush leather chair and offered a handshake. His shock of white hair meant he was over seventy.

"Robert Eckerman, at your service. I'm semi retired. Don't have much of a staff, I'm afraid."

We assured him we just wanted a few minutes of his time.

"I'm Meera Patel and this is Tony Sinclair," I began. "We are from a small town called Swan Creek in Oklahoma."

His jovial expression turned serious and he asked us to go on.

"A friend of ours was found dead a few days ago."

I wanted to make sure this man knew Charlie Gibson before launching into the whole story. Otherwise it was just a waste of everyone's time.

"Are you talking about Charlie Gibson?" he asked immediately.

I nodded.

"I had been trying to reach him for some time. A woman named Audrey finally answered his phone. She told me what happened. It's so sad. I bailed Leo out as soon as I heard."

"So you know Leo too?" I burst out.

"Sure do. He's my client. Or has been for a long time, in a way."

Tony and I stared at each other. Could it be this man wasn't aware of Leo's fate?

"Leo found your visiting card among Charlie's stuff. We are on a road trip to the coast. It's Spring Break, you know."

Eckerman nodded encouragingly.

"Leo asked if we might stop to say Hi since Barstow is on our way."

"That kid should have called me by now, especially if he found the letter I sent to Charlie."

I must have looked blank.

"My card was stapled to the letter I sent Charlie Gibson. I am thinking if he found the card, he found the letter."

I just nodded a yes.

"Do you know why he hasn't called me back?"

Barstow looked like a small place. Apparently, the news hadn't reached the local papers.

"Er, yes!" I murmured, feeling tongue tied.

My eyes welled up and Robert Eckerman leaned forward, sensing something was wrong.

"He's alright, isn't he?"

"Leo was found dead five days ago," Tony cut in. "He left a note confessing to killing Charlie. The police deemed his death a suicide."

"That poor boy! What do *you* think?" he stared at us.

"Leo's innocent," I flared up. "I believed that from day one. The police are finally beginning to think so too."

Robert Eckerman sat stunned in his leather armchair. He looked his age.

"Leo had a lot to live for. There's no way he would commit suicide. Not if he read the letter I sent Charlie Gibson."

"He mentioned some possible good news," I said, staring at Eckerman. "Do you know what he was talking about?"

"It's a long story," Eckerman sighed. "Can I get you anything before we begin?"

I asked for some water and he pulled a cold bottle out of a small refrigerator.

"I'm originally from Dallas. I had a big firm and wealthy clients. I moved here after I retired. My kids live in LA and I like to visit the casinos. This place is kind of in between, the best of both worlds."

"So you have clients from Texas and surrounding states?" I read between the lines.

"You're a smart one," he smiled. "I took over this practice from my Dad. We have some clients that go back generations. My Dad handled their estates and I handle the estates of their descendants."

I tried to guess what was coming.

"One such client was Leonard Cunningham. He made a lot of money in oil, millions. He had the Midas touch in business, but his personal life wasn't that great."

It was a common story. Rich people often ignore their families.

"He had a falling out with his son. Son wanted to be in the movies. He left home and came to California. Met a girl here, another wannabe starlet. They married pretty young."

"Did he ever go back?"

Eckerman shook his head.

"Leonard Cunningham's wife died. The son blamed her death on the father. Their rift deepened. Leonard got a trophy wife, a woman much younger than him. He wanted more kids."

"What about the son?"

"He had a daughter. They got some small parts in movies, and managed to raise the girl. Disaster struck again and the daughter became a teen mom."

"Seems like they had a lot of bad luck," I clucked. "What about the trophy wife?"

"She never had any kids. Leonard grew old and eccentric, and died pining for the grandchild he never met."

The story was sad alright. Where did Leo come in?

"I'm coming to it," Eckerman said, reading my mind. "Leonard's granddaughter was a spunky one. She had the baby and continued her education. Her parents helped her raise the child. The child was called Leo after his great grandpa."

"Leo said he got his name from his birth month."

"That's probably what he was told," Eckerman said moodily.

"Some time when the child was eight, they all got into a car accident. Only the child survived. He was shuffled around to some group homes, sent to foster families. Two years ago, he ran away."

"Why did he do that?"

"Hard to say, Meera. Some foster parents are abusive. The kids are really better off on their own. And teenagers are moody. We don't know who was at fault."

"So Leo was on the run for a while. And then he met Charlie."

"Charlie Gibson seems to have been good to the boy."

"He was," I confirmed. "He wasn't too touchy feely from what I gather. But Leo had a safe place to live in, and he was well fed. He was a happy kid. He was looking forward to college."

Eckerman blinked, and looked away.

"I suppose you are wondering what my connection to Leo is?"

I almost screamed yes.

"Leonard Cunningham was a wily one. He created a trust for his next of kin. His new wife had use of his estate for life. Everything went to his great grandchild after that."

"Did his son know all this?"

"He did. But he was stubborn. He didn't want any of it."

"Not even for Leo?"

"They might have told Leo about it when he got older. But then everything fell apart."

"What if Leo didn't want this money?"

"As long as there was an heir, Leonard's second wife didn't have control over anything. But she got it all in the absence of one. She could leave it to anyone she wanted, or just give it all to charity."

"Why did you start looking for Leo?"

"Leo's eighteenth birthday was coming up. According to our instructions, we were to contact him once and tell him about his inheritance. I initiated the process six months before the date, like we usually do. That's when I learned Leo was on the run."

"So he had access to all this money, but he was still homeless."

Nothing made sense to me.

"Once Leonard's son and granddaughter declined the inheritance, our instructions were to wait until the baby came of age."

"How did you find Leo?"

"It wasn't easy," Eckerman said grimly. "I hired investigators. It was easy enough to trace him through the system. But the trail went cold once he was on the run."

"Did Charlie ever get back to you?"

"He called me once. He wanted to confirm someone wasn't playing a joke on them. He said Leo had some test coming up. He was going to surprise him with the news after that."

"Were you surprised Leo was all the way across the country in Oklahoma?"

"It was ironic, that's what it was."

"How so?"

"Guess where Leonard Cunningham spent the last years of his life?"

I didn't have the patience for any guessing games. My face must have shown that because Eckerman answered his own question right away.

"Swan Creek, Meera. Your town."

"Can't say I've heard of him."

"He died before you were born," Eckerman said. "His wife lives on his estate."

"You know her then?"

"Rose Cunningham got rid of us the moment her husband died. She wasn't happy she only got the income from her husband's estate. She didn't want Leonard's old advisors interfering with her lifestyle."

"Did she know about Leo?"

Eckerman shrugged.

"I guess the information was out there for anyone who wanted to find it. But she wouldn't know we were supposed to contact Leo when he turned 18."

"This is a lot to process, Mr. Eckerman."

"Who gets all the money now that Leo is dead?" Tony asked.

"I'm afraid it will all revert to Rose Cunningham now."

"Do you realize what that means?" I banged my fist on the table in excitement.

Tony and Eckerman stared at me.

"We finally have a motive for Leo's murder! And Charlie's too."

"I suppose there's no other reason anyone would have wanted Leo out of the way?"

"No, Mr. Eckerman, there isn't!"

I was feeling confident about this.

"Would you be willing to talk to the Swan Creek police?"

Eckerman agreed and I asked for the use of his phone. Stan Miller came on the line and I told him the fantastic story I had just heard.

"We haven't been idle either, Meera. It's all beginning to come together now."

Chapter 30

I'm less than generous while talking about the Swan Creek police. But they come through when needed. Stan gave us a brief report on what they had been up to for the last couple of days.

"You know that sand bothered me, Meera."

We were all listening to Stan on the speaker phone.

"We posted a man there, outside the gates. We observed a few people coming in and out of the Palms frequently. One of them was a landscaping van. This man, a local guy we know, confirmed they have that kind of sand by their lake. He got us a sample. It's being tested right now, compared against the stuff we found on Leo's shoes."

"Does anyone named Rose Cunningham live there?"

I just wanted to confirm it, inspite of what Eckerman had said.

"The Cunningham estate is one of the largest inside the Palms. The old lady who lives there is kind of whacko. Her nephew lives there with her."

"How do you know that, Stan? We just told you about the Cunninghams."

"We have eyes and ears everywhere, Meera," Stan said pompously. "Let's say Doug Martin has raised a few flags."

"Who's Doug Martin?"

"Keep up, Meera! That's Rose Cunningham's nephew."

"Go on!"

"Leo's death has been talked about a lot in the papers. Almost everyone in town has heard about it. We showed his picture to the guards at the Palms. They admitted Leo came there the day he died."

"What happens now?"

"All this time, we were trying to find a connection between Leo and someone at the Palms. Now that we know he is a Cunningham, things will be much easier."

Stan promised to keep us posted and hung up.

Robert Eckerman cleared his throat.

"I am willing to bet Rose and her nephew are involved in this. Will you keep me in the loop?"

We shook hands again, and Tony and I stepped out of the law office. I was in shock. Life is so fickle. We really don't know what's waiting for us around the bend. If only Charlie had told Leo about Eckerman's letter the moment he got it? Would they both have been alive right now?

The family was waiting for us impatiently. We had been away for over an hour. Motee Ba had packed a couple of subs for us.

"Everything alright?" she asked, sensing my mood.

I looked at Dad. I wasn't sure he would want to hear about all this. It might spoil the mood.

"Speak up, girl," Pappa boomed, tapping his cane. "Was this about Charlie Gibson?"

I gave them a high level version. Everyone looked shocked. We piled into the car and set off toward the last point in our journey. I could see Motee Ba's lips move silently in the rearview mirror. I was sure she was saying a prayer for Leo.

Tony switched on the radio and I closed my eyes, thinking about what must be happening back in Swan Creek. The folks in the back must have dozed off. The traffic increased as we got closer to cities. Barely an hour later, Pappa made his usual demand for lunch.

"It's 1:30," Pappa said. "Past my lunch time."

There was a discussion on whether we should drive on straight to Sally's home and order something there or stop on the way.

"Your mother's tired just like the rest of us," Motee Ba warned. "We are not going to make her work soon as we get home."

"Let's stop somewhere along the way," Dad reasoned. "I'm a bit hungry too, actually."

It turned out everyone wanted lunch. Tony entered a city and stopped outside a Mexican restaurant. Motee Ba's words made sense. Sally had been living with us in Swan Creek for the past few weeks. We would probably need to hit a grocery store first for milk and juice.

The food in California had its own taste. I had never given much thought to enchiladas before this. Now that I had eaten them in New Mexico, Arizona and California, I had a new appreciation for how versatile they could be.

"How far is the beach from your place, Mom?" Jeet asked, biting into a giant burrito.

"About thirty minutes," Sally answered.

"Have you ever gone surfing?" he asked her.

Sally smiled. That meant a yes.

"Leave your mother alone," Dad ordered.

I sneaked a look at my watch. It had been about two hours since we spoke to Stan. I wondered if there had been any more developments.

"Do you want to call Stan Miller?" Dad asked.

I felt like a deer caught in the headlights.

"Take my phone," Dad said, handing over his cell phone.

He couldn't have shocked me more if he had handed me a $100 bill. Sally patted his arm and smiled. This must be her idea.

I got up from the table, having lost all interest in the flan. I almost jogged outside as I dialed Stan.

"Hey Stan! It's Meera."

"It's over, Meera. We got him."

"Tell me everything," I gushed. "Don't leave anything out."

Tony had come out behind me. We got into the car and I put the phone on speaker.

"Doug Martin confessed to killing Charlie Gibson and Leo Smith."

"Was it all for the Cunningham fortune?"

"You better believe it."

"Does he get this money now?"

With access to millions of dollars, Doug Martin could hire the best lawyers and even get away with his crime.

"That depends on his aunt, Rose Cunningham."

"But how did you get him to confess?"

"Things moved pretty fast after we talked last, Meera. We showed a photo of Doug Martin around. Both Audrey and Joyce Baker recognized him. He had paid some visits to Charlie in the last couple of months."

"But Eckerman sent Charlie that letter two weeks ago."

"It's like this. Rose Cunningham hired Doug Martin to take care of the estate. He lived with her and acted like an estate manager. She led him to believe he was going to inherit everything after her."

"But that wasn't true!"

"Right! This lady kept Doug on a short leash, dangling her money like a carrot. She fell ill about a year ago. Actually, she's counting her last days now. Somehow, she let it slip Doug wasn't getting squat after she was gone."

"I bet that didn't go down well."

"As I said before, that Martin guy's a shady character anyway. He's had a lot of spare cash and plenty of time on his hands. He got used to the posh life, being a lord of the manor and all that."

"Go on, Stan!" I urged, getting impatient.

"Martin hired investigators to find out where this kid was. Once he knew the kid was missing, he began to believe he must be dead. But then the investigation turned up a nasty surprise. Not only was the kid alive, he was right there under his nose in Swan Creek."

"And Leo had no idea about all this!"

"Martin kept a watch on Charlie Gibson, sort of got to know him. Said he was a sly one. He didn't let Martin get close."

"Sounds like Charlie alright."

"Martin turned up at places Charlie went to. He took morning walks at Willow Springs, went to the library and the grocery store. Charlie began to trust him. He proposed some kind of scheme."

"Scheme for what?"

"He just wanted to get into Charlie's home. The plan was simple. He was going to kill Charlie and blame it all on Leo. Leo would go to jail and he would run away with the money."

"But Leo would catch up to it sometime?"

"Martin knew Leo had no idea he was a Cunningham. That was part of why he had befriended Charlie. To get all the information on Leo."

"Then Eckerman started looking for Leo."

"Martin had no idea about that. He didn't know about Leo's bail. But Leo turned up at his door."

"Eckerman's letter! He never actually said what was in it."

"He must have mentioned Rose Cunningham. Or maybe Charlie wrote it down somewhere. The kid figured it out. He was excited to find out he had family."

"But Rose wasn't exactly his family."

"I don't think he saw it that way. He just found out he had family, after being alone all this time."

"It must have meant more to Leo than all that money."

"That's what he said to the old lady. Martin says she had no idea about all this. She's gone soft in her death bed, according to him."

"Nasty man," I fumed.

"He's nasty alright. He saw all the money slip through his fingers when Leo turned up at the Cunningham estate. He hatched a plan while Leo was talking to Rose. He took him for a tour of the property. He dropped sleeping pills in some lemonade and handed Leo the drink as he showed him around. Leo drank it all without any suspicion."

"And he staged the suicide too, I guess."

"Martin knew when Audrey left. Charlie's house was empty. He could have dumped Leo anywhere but the car was a problem. So he drove Leo back to Charlie's, and made it look like he wrote a note and took those pills."

"Leo never saw it coming."

"Apparently not! Martin says Leo was very happy when he took his last breath."

I felt the tears slide down my cheeks. Leo had been better off homeless.

"We need to give Leo a proper farewell," I spoke through my tears.

"You were a good friend to him, Meera," Stan said. "You fought for him even when the odds were stacked against you."

"What will Rose do now?"

"It's up to her. She gets it all but she doesn't have much time to enjoy any of it."

I hung up, feeling a wave of emotion overcome me. Tony made me go wash up in the restroom. Everyone was waiting eagerly for an update. I couldn't speak. Tony gave them a brief version of Stan's story.

"Poor Charlie!" Pappa whispered, trying to control himself.

Dad paid up and we shuffled out. Each of us was trying to process the story in their own way.

Chapter 31

The silence in the car was palpable. Even Jeet seemed to have processed everything finally. We drove through the Angeles National Forest as I-15 wound south further into California.

"Where are we going exactly?" I asked Dad.

"You'll see," he said.

Sally was driving. I suppose she didn't need any directions to go home. We were literally at her mercy. I speculated about what new hell we might encounter at the other end. I am generally not this pessimistic but the Leo tragedy had put a pall over things. All the fun we had in the past week had faded into oblivion.

Sally merged onto a local highway and we entered Pasadena after a while. We drove through Glendale and saw signs for Hollywood. Jeet was beginning to perk up. Tony and Jeet both let out a whoop when we saw the Hollywood sign. Sally drove on and finally entered the city of Beverly Hills.

"You live in 90210?" I asked.

She gave me one of her smiles, barely taking her eyes off the road.

Like any teen of my generation, I had been a big fan of Beverly Hills 90210, the teen soap that ruled television for the past decade. I still had a poster of Jason Priestly in my room. I had wished I had a convertible in high school, just like Kelly from the show.

I had assumed Sally was loaded, but her wealth suddenly took on new perspective. She lived in one of the most coveted zip codes in the country. she probably jostled elbows with film stars.

Sally finally slowed on a tree lined street and drove into what seemed like a tall hedge. It was the entrance to a driveway. The car went around a curve and stopped in front of a sprawling Spanish style house. Two giant concrete urns overflowed with flowers, guarding an impeccable emerald lawn. The intricately carved wooden door burst open and a woman bustled out. She was in her 50s, with a mop of curly salt and pepper hair, dressed in a maid's uniform.

"Miss Sally!" she cried. "You're home."

Sally jumped down from the car and hugged the woman. She lapsed into Spanish and chattered away. None of us had budged from our seats. Sally finally turned around and motioned us to come out.

"This is Bianca," she told Dad. "She takes care of us."

Bianca shyly said Hello to all of us. Pappa was looking a bit dazed. His eyes whirled around, taking in the details of the house. A smaller building lay to a side, and I assumed it was a guest house. Sally ushered everyone in and the boys started helping Bianca with the bags.

We went into a big, comfortably furnished living room. I collapsed into an overstuffed chair and began closing my eyes. A patch of blue swam before my eyes and I sat up with a jerk.

"Is that a pool?" I burst out, sounding like Jeet.

Sally nodded, looking pleased.

"Let me show you around."

There were five bedrooms in the house, with one master suite on the first floor. I supposed that belonged to Sally. She put us kids in the guest house.

"How long have you lived here?" I asked.

"Ten years," Sally said.

Her fake husband must have been doctor to the stars or something similar. Or he had been dealing drugs. How else could he have afforded this mansion? Sally's wardrobe didn't seem surprising anymore. She probably shopped on Rodeo Drive.

"Miss Sally," Bianca called out eagerly. "I have your favorite fajitas ready to go on the grill."

"Thank you, Bianca. We'll all have some now."

No one wanted to say no to fajitas. I wiped my plate and licked my fingers clean after polishing off a big platter. Bianca's fajitas surpassed mine. I vowed to pick up a few tips from her.

We adjourned to the guest house with our bags. Although we had just gorged on the fajitas, I was craving something sweet. I raided the fridge in the guest house and found a tray of cupcakes.

"Who do you think these are for?" I asked the boys.

"Let me ask Mom," Jeet volunteered.

He used the intercom in the kitchen to call the main house. His laugh rolled over me, reminding me of how Leo would never laugh again.

"We can eat them," Jeet said, hanging up. "Mom asked Bianca to make them for you. She knows you like to eat in the middle of the night."

"I like no such thing!"

"How about a swim later?" Tony stepped in. "Have you seen that pool?"

An engine roared outside and we rushed to the windows, peering outside. The car was fire engine red and it almost hugged the ground. The driver idled in front of a garage and flipped a button. The door began rising up slowly. The driver impatiently floored the gas pedal, and the car finally shot into the tiny space.

"What in blazes…" I muttered.

Did Sally have another house guest we didn't know about?

A door slammed and a skimpily dressed young girl got out. Her cut off shorts barely covered her butt. Large oversized sunglasses covered her eyes. She took off the glasses and squinted at the LX in the middle of the driveway.

Her face looked vaguely familiar and a feeling of déjà vu passed over me. she spotted us standing in the window and started walking toward us.

I saw Dad and Sally hurry out of the front door, just before I turned around.

Tony had rushed forward and flung the door open.

"Hola hermanos!" the girl chortled. "How was your drive?"

High school Spanish had never been my strong point. Jeet always aced it though. His face had turned green.

"Why aren't you in school, Cristina?" A stern voice called from the door. "And what were you thinking, taking the car out by yourself?"

I had never seen Sally look so formidable.

"Hola Mama!" the girl cried, and tottered over to hug Sally.

Sally's face softened for a moment as she let herself be hugged.

"Bianca said you were visiting. So here I am."

Dad had come inside by then. He stood next to me, holding my arm.

"Why don't we all sit down?" he said in his professor's voice.

"Mom?" Jeet asked fearfully. "Why is she calling you Mama?"

I connected the dots before Sally opened her mouth.

"Jeet, Meera, this is Cristina, your baby sister."

Cristina lunged toward us, folding Jeet and me in a bear hug.

"I'm so happy to meet you at last."

Dad refused to meet my eye as my gaze bore into him. He must have known about this for some time. Why had no one thought to give us some warning?

"How old are you?" I asked, trying to hide my shock.

"Fifteen," she chirped. "Almost nine years younger than you,

Meera."

She turned toward Jeet.

"I always wanted an older brother."

My eyes met Sally's over her head. They were brimming over with unshed tears. I don't know how much Sally really remembered about her past life but she had accepted us as family.

I was the only one holding back.

Glossary

Desi – broadly refers to people from the Indian subcontinent

Gujarati – of the Indian state of Gujarat; pertaining to people from the western Indian state of Gujarat

Ba – Mother

Motee Ba – Grandma, literally Big Ma – pronounced with a hard T like in T-shirt

Thepla – a flatbread made with wheat flour, pan fried. Chopped fenugreek leaves are often added to the dough along with spices like turmeric and coriander.

Gadhedo – ass; used as an expletive

Chevdo – snack mix made with seasoned rice flakes

Laddu – Indian dessert made with clarified butter, flour and sugar, rolled into a ball.

Dhebra – Gujarati snack made with millet flour, seasoned with tamarind and sesame seeds and deep fried. It has a chewy texture and earthy taste.

Bhel – popular Indian street food snack, made with puffed rice, fried snack mixes and many condiments.

Khichdi – stew made with rice and lentils

RECIPE - Masala Chai/ Chai Latte

Ingredients

1.5 cups water

1 cup milk

¼ tsp Tea Masala (see below)

2 tsp tea powder or 2 tea bags

Method

Add milk and water to a sauce pan.

Add in the spices or spice mix. Bring to a boil.

When mixture boils, simmer for a minute so that spices are infused.

Lower heat and add tea powder or tea bags.

Boil for 2-3 minutes until the mixture changes color. Boil more for a stronger tea.

Drain and serve immediately.

Add sugar according to taste.

Tea Masala Spice – Available in online stores or Indian stores as a spice mix. You can make your own for 2-4 cups of tea. Take 1 green cardamom pod, 1 clove, 3 white peppercorns and crush them in a mortar. Add this to the milk/ water mixture along with ¼ tsp ground ginger. You have your very own fresh tea masala or spice mix.

RECIPE - Vegetable Puffs

Ingredients

1 cup green peas

1 cup boiled, cubed potatoes

½ tsp crushed garlic and grated ginger

¼ tsp minced jalapeno (optional)

¼ tsp garam masala or curry powder

1 tsp oil

Salt to taste

4-6 puff pastry sheets

Method

Blanch the green peas and drain completely. Pulse in food processor until coarsely ground.

Heat oil in a pan.

Add in ginger/garlic/chili and immediately add the peas. Fry for a few seconds. Then add in the spices and the potatoes. Switch off heat.

Mash until well mixed. Cool completely.

Slightly roll out the puff pastry sheet and cut into 3-4 parts, about 3 inch by 3 inch.

Place a spoonful of the veggie mixture in the center. Bring together the ends and seal to join in a triangle or rectangle shape. Bake these puffs in a 350F oven for 10-15 minutes until golden brown.

Serve hot with sauce of choice.

RECIPE - Avocado Chili Salad

Ingredients

2 ripe avocados

4-6 ripe tomatoes

2 green chilies – jalapeno, Hatch etc.

1-2 limes, juiced

2 Tbsp honey

8 oz Queso Fresco, cubed

2 Tbsp cilantro, chopped

Salt and pepper to taste

Drizzle of olive oil (optional)

Method

Chop avocados and cover with lime juice to prevent oxidation.

Chop tomatoes in similar sized chunks and add to avocado

Mince or chop chilies (use jalapeno or poblano if you don't have Hatch chili)

Add the cilantro, cheese, salt and pepper, honey and olive oil.

Toss lightly.

Serve immediately or refrigerate.

RECIPE - Chili Honey Corn

Ingredients

4 corns on the cob

½ cup green chili sauce/ salsa

1 lime juiced

½ cup olive oil

¼ -1/2 cup honey

Salt to taste

½ cup goat cheese

Method

Mix the chili sauce, oil, honey and salt to form a marinade.

Grill the corn on a hot gas stove or grill. When almost cooked from all sides, slather the marinade on the corn and grill for a minute or two more.

Serve with fresh lime wedges and goat's cheese crumbled on top.

RECIPE - Bhel Poori

Ingredients

6-8 cups puffed rice (murmura)

1 cup sev (Indian fried noodles)

1 cup farsan or mixture

1 cup onion, diced fine

1 cup tomatoes, diced fine

1 cup boiled potatoes, cubed

¼ cup cilantro, diced fine

1-2 jalapeno peppers, minced

¼ tsp cumin, ground

½ tsp Chat masala

½-1 cup sweet date tamarind chutney

Salt to taste

Method

Mix all the ingredients in a bowl. Serve immediately.

Note – potatoes should be cold. You can also make a paste of cilantro and jalapenos and use it instead of the minced version.

Ethnic ingredients are easily available in Indian grocery stores or online retailers like Amazon.

Join my Newsletter

Get access to exclusive bonus content, sneak peeks, giveaways and much more. Also get a chance to join my exclusive ARC group, the people who get first dibs at all my new books.

Sign up at the following link and join the fun.

Click here → **http://www.subscribepage.com/leenaclovernl**

Limited time – A Bonus Chapter from Gone With the Wings FREE when you sign up (deleted scenes)

Get in touch -

Leenaclover@gmail.com

http://twitter.com/leenaclover

https://www.facebook.com/meerapatelcozymystery

Thank You

Thank you so much for reading *Back to the Fajitas*.

I had a great time writing this book and I hope you enjoyed reading it.

If you enjoyed the book, **please consider writing a review**.

Your feedback helps me get better at what I do. It is also a great way to let other cozy mystery readers know what you thought of the book.

Every review you write makes a **big** difference in many ways.

This is the best way to support me and my craft so that I can continue this and bring you more such books.

Thanks again for spending time with Meera and family. Hope to see you again soon.

~ Author Leena Clover

Leenaclover@gmail.com

http://twitter.com/leenaclover

https://www.facebook.com/meerapatelcozymystery

Books by Leena Clover

Gone with the Wings – Meera Patel Cozy Mystery Book 1
https://www.amazon.com/dp/B071WHNM6K

A Pocket Full of Pie - Meera Patel Cozy Mystery Book 2
https://www.amazon.com/dp/B072Q7B47P/

For a Few Dumplings More - Meera Patel Cozy Mystery Book 3
https://www.amazon.com/dp/B072V3T2BV

Back to the Fajitas - Meera Patel Cozy Mystery Book 4
https://www.amazon.com/dp/B0748KPTLM